Rebuilding Coventry

SUE TOWNSEND

Rebuilding Coventry

A Tale of Two Cities

Methuen

544490

First published in Great Britain 1988
by Methuen London
Michelin House, 81 Fulham Road, London SW3 6RB
Copyright © Sue Townsend 1988

British Library Cataloguing in Publication Data

Townsend, Sue
  Rebuilding Coventry.
  I. Title
  823'.914 [F]
    ISBN 0-413-54240-8

Printed and bound in Great Britain
by Richard Clay Ltd, Bungay, Suffolk

To Geoffrey Strachan – he knows why

Contents

1 Yesterday I Killed a Man

There are two things that you should know about me immediately: the first is that I am beautiful, the second is that yesterday I killed a man called Gerald Fox. Both things were accidents. My parents are not good-looking. My father looks like a tennis ball, bald and round, and my mother closely resembles a bread knife, thin, jagged and with a cutting tongue. I have never liked them and I suspect they don't like me.

And, I neither loved nor hated Gerald Fox enough to want to kill him.

But I love my brother Sidney, and I think he loves me. We laugh together about Tennis Ball and Bread Knife. Sidney is married to a sad woman called Ruth. Ruth sighs before she speaks, and when she has finished speaking she sighs again. Sighs are her punctuation marks. Sidney is besotted with her: he finds her melancholia to be deeply erotic. They have no children, and don't want any. Ruth claims to be too afraid of the world, and Sidney wants frightened Ruth all to himself. They make love seven times a week – more if the weather's hot – and when they go abroad they hardly leave their hotel room. Sidney tells me nearly everything about his marriage, although he is surprisingly squeamish about money. 'No, no,' he says, and shudders away from financial talk.

He is a sales manager in a store selling electrical goods in the city where we were both born, a dab hand at selling cameras, compact disc players and portable colour televisions to people who can't afford them. Sidney is successful because, like me, he is beautiful. He has a smile that customers can't resist. They are hypnotized by the deep brown of his eyes, and the lush growth of his eyelashes. As they sign the credit arrangement they admire his hands. They don't mind when he tells them that the consumer durable they have just purchased, and want immediately, will not be delivered for a fortnight. They are too busy listening to his heartbreaking voice with its charming hesitations and throaty catches. They leave the shop in a daze. One woman walked backwards out of the shop still waving to

Sidney and backed onto a motorbike which carried her fifteen yards before throwing her into the gutter. Other people in the shop ran out to help her but Sidney stayed inside to guard the till.

Sidney has a very cold heart. He has never suffered himself and is irritated by other people's pain. He has refused to watch the television news 'since they started clogging it up with films of bloody famine victims'. I once asked Sidney what he wanted out of life. 'Nothing,' he said. 'I've already got it.' He was thirty-two then. I said: 'But what will you do until you die?' He laughed and said: 'Make more money and buy more things.' My brother is pragmatic to a fault. He doesn't know I killed a man yesterday. He's on holiday in a villa on the Algarve and he won't answer the telephone.

Sidney is the only person in the world I know who won't be shocked that I am wanted by the police. I am almost pleased that he has no principles; unprincipled people are a great comfort in times of crisis.

I have an unusual Christian name: Coventry. My father was visiting Coventry on the day I was born. He was delivering a lorry-load of sand to a bomb-site. 'Thank God he wasn't on an errand to Giggleswick,' my mother used to say at least three times a week. It is the nearest she has come to cracking a joke in the whole of her life.

Sidney was also named after a city: my father saw a picture of Sydney Harbour Bridge in *Tit Bits* and fell in love with it. He knew its weight and length and the frequency with which it was painted.

When I grew up I was puzzled at these quixotic choices. With the cold eye of adolescence I saw that my father was stultifyingly dull and possessed no imagination whatsoever.

Naturally Sidney and I have always hated our names. I longed to be an anonymous Pat, Susan or Ann, and Sidney wanted to be called Steve. But then every man I've ever known has wanted to be called Steve.

So there you are. I have an extraordinary face, body and name, but unfortunately I am a very ordinary woman with no obvious talents, no influential family connections, no qualifications in anything at all and no income. Yesterday I had a husband and two teenage children. Today I am alone, I'm on the run and I'm in London, *without my handbag.*

2 A Night Out with the Neighbours

They had been sitting in the pub, Coventry Dakin and her friends. It was Monday evening. Coventry was not enjoying herself. Derek, her husband, had raised his voice to her before she left home. He was going out to the Annual General Meeting of the Tortoise Society and he thought that Coventry should stay in with the children.

'But Derek, they're sixteen and seventeen, old enough to be left,' whispered Coventry.

'And what if a gang of violent yobs decide to break in and beat John up and rape Mary?' Derek hissed. Neither of them believed in arguing in front of the children, so they were in the back garden in the tortoise shed. Outside was the glooming night. Derek had picked up a lettuce during his last speech and was carefully peeling away leaves and feeding them to his beloved tortoises. Coventry could hear their shells clacking together as they rushed towards Derek's hand.

'But there aren't any violent gangs around here, Derek,' she said.

'Those gangs drive round in *cars*, Coventry. They come out of the inner city and pick on affluent suburban houses.'

'But this is a council estate, Derek.'

'But we're buying *our* house, aren't we?'

'How would a car-load of yobs know that?'

'Because of the Georgian doors and windows I've put in, of course. But if you want to leave John and Mary alone and defenceless, then go ahead. Go out drinking with your common friends.'

Coventry didn't defend her friends against this charge because they were, undeniably, common.

'Anyway, I don't like to think of you sitting in a pub.' He was sulking now; Coventry could just make out his pushed-up bottom lip in the dark.

'*Don't* think about it, then. Concentrate on your slimy tortoises.' She was almost shouting.

'Tortoises are not slimy, as you would know if you could ever bring yourself to touch one.'

There was a long silence between man and wife which was broken only by the surprisingly loud crunching noises made by the feasting tortoises. For something to do Coventry read the beasts' names, which Derek had written immaculately in fluorescent paint on each shell: 'Ruth', 'Naomi', 'Jacob' and 'Job'.

'Shouldn't they be hibernating?' she asked her husband.

This was a sore point. There had already been several frosts but Derek kept putting off the evil day. The truth was that he always missed them during the long winter months.

'Allow *me* to decide on a suitable date for their hibernation, will you?' said Derek. But he thought to himself, 'Must get some straw on my way home from work tomorrow.'

Derek was worried. A series of disastrous summers had put his pets off their food, thus leaving them short of body fats and jeopardizing their chances of surviving their winter sojourn in dreamland. He'd tried force-feeding them but had stopped when they'd shown obvious signs of distress. He now weighed them daily, noting their respective weights in an exercise book. He blamed himself for not noticing their anorexic condition earlier, though how he was supposed to see through their thick shells he didn't know. He didn't have X-ray vision, did he?

'Now, if you don't mind?' Derek had held the shed door open for Coventry. She had squeezed past him through the narrow opening, not wanting to touch or be touched by him, and walked across the dark, damp grass where the tortoises sported during the summer months, and went into the house.

The pub Coventry and her friends were sitting in was called Astaire's. It was a theme pub. The theme being the cinematic persona of Fred Astaire. The brewery's designer had razed the old name, the Black Pig, from the exterior and the sturdy wooden tables and comfortable bench seating from the interior. Drinkers were now forced to crouch over pink and chromium coffee-tables. Their large bums lapped over the edges of tiny, pink Dralon stools. The refurbishment was meant to represent a nineteen-thirties Hollywood night-club, but the clientele remained stubbornly unsophisticated; spurning all inducements to buy cocktails, preferring to swig beer from straight glasses.

Fred Astaire costumes had been provided for the bar staff, who had worn them for the first week until, irritated beyond endurance by the inconvenience of wearing top hats, starched collars and tailcoats, they had rebelled and reverted to wearing their own clothes.

Greta, sixteen stone and a barmaid at the Black Pig since leaving school, had resigned as soon as last orders were called on the night of the reopening.

'I looked a right bleddy prat in a top 'at,' she said outside on the pavement.

'You did an' all, Greta,' said one regular, who had missed looking at her comfortable cleavage.

It took Derek a full five minutes to settle Ruth, Naomi, Jacob and Job down for the night and then another few minutes to bolt and padlock the windows and door of the shed. Tortoises are now rare and valuable animals and tortoise-rustling is all too common in Britain. So Derek took no chances. He didn't know what he would do if his quartet of animals were stolen from him. Apart from loving them, he could never afford to restock. When he went back into the house he found that Coventry had disobeyed him and gone to the pub.

'I've *got* to go out, sorry, but it's the Annual General Meeting,' he explained to his indifferent children. 'Will you be all right?'

'Course,' they said.

When the Georgian door had slammed behind Derek, the children opened a bottle of their father's elderflower wine and settled down, drink in hand, to watch a semi-pornographic video called *Vile Bodies*.

Because of the row with Derek, Coventry was ill at ease. To make things worse one of those conversational voids had occurred. To fill it she gabbled the first thing that came into her head. 'How old was Jesus when he died?' she asked.

'For Christ's sake!' Greta rasped in her sixty-a-day voice. 'I've come here to enjoy myself, not to have a bleedin' religious discussion!' Coventry blushed, then tried very hard to stop blushing. She had read that day that with positive thinking your body could be made to do anything.

'He didn't *die*, he was murdered,' said Maureen, who was thin and careful about detail.

'He was thirty-three,' said Greta in a hostile, warning tone. She clicked her handbag shut with an air of finality.

Coventry looked at Greta and thought that she was a bully. She imagined Greta's big, squashy body wearing skinhead clothes instead of her usual polyester afternoon frocks and the picture inside her head made her smirk. A hairy man with sideburns who was lounging with his back against the bar smirked back at her, so Coventry quickly looked away and pretended to search through her handbag for something.

Maureen laughed quietly and said, 'Eh, it looks like Cov's clicked. That bloke in the overalls just smiled at her.'

Greta lit a cigarette and, through an exhalation of dirty smoke, said: 'That's Norman Parker. He's a compulsive gambler and he's got the worst-smelling feet of any man I've ever known. Keep clear of him, Cov.'

The three women looked at Norman Parker's feet hidden inside industrial boots. Noticing their glance, Norman shouted: 'You wouldn't know me when I'm washed and done up. Cecil Parkinson's got nowt on me.'

Mr Patel, the landlord, looked up from the microwave where mysterious rays were warming a shepherd's pie for Norman's supper. He didn't like raised voices in his pub. In his experience raised voices were a prelude to calling the police, before locking himself in the stock-room with the contents of the till.

Gerald Fox crashed into the bar from the street and stood looking around importantly, as though he were about to announce the outbreak of war. 'Bung us a sausage roll in the micro, Abdul,' he shouted. Mr Patel whispered bitter words under his breath. He hated to be called Abdul. Why couldn't this man learn to pronounce his given name properly? Was Parvez too difficult for his clumsy tongue?

'Would you like anything else, Mr Fox?' enquired Mr Patel.

'Well, Abdul, I wouldn't mind a night with your missus. I've heard that she's some goer.' Gerald laughed long and hard, and Norman Parker joined in to be sociable.

But Mr Patel was not smiling. After the laughter had died away he said: 'You have been misinformed, Mr Fox. You must have been told that my wife was *from* Goa, as indeed she is. Goa was her place of birth; it is a small territory next to the Indian Ocean.'

The ping of the microwave called him away. Coventry laughed and clapped her hands and exchanged smiles with Mr Patel. Gerald looked over his shoulder and shouted: 'Well, if it's not Coventry

Tittie . . . sorry, I mean City.' Once again Norman Parker echoed Gerald's laughter. His mouth opened and closed, displaying half-chewed bits of shepherd's pie. Gerald turned his back and ordered a pint.

Maureen said, 'Shall we move on somewhere else, girls?'

Greta said, 'No, why should we? We was here first.' Then, to Gerald Fox, 'If I had a mouth like yours I'd donate it to the Channel Tunnel project.'

Norman Parker, always obliging, laughed. Gerald turned, took a deep drink of lager and said threateningly: 'Now then, Greta.'

Coventry was still blushing to the roots of her naturally blonde hair at Gerald Fox's allusion to her breasts. She folded her arms over them, as she had done millions of times since the first schoolboy had shouted 'Coventry Tittie!' in the street twenty-seven years ago.

Norman and Gerald were talking at the bar, swopping lies and bragging about money earned, personal strength and women con-quered. *Gerald told Norman the terrible lie that Coventry had been his mistress for over a year.* He elaborated: 'I see her on Mondays, Wednesdays and Saturdays, but the rest of the time we have to pretend that we don't get on.'

Norman said, 'Well, she had me fooled. To be quite honest, I thought she looked like she hated you.'

Gerald lowered his voice. 'She's crazy about me, always on at me to leave my missus, but I said to her only last Wednesday, I said: "Coventry, don't ask me to leave my kids; it would kill me." '

Norman Parker nodded sympathetically. He had left his kids two years ago and now, made maudlin with drink, he briefly regretted it.

'I live opposite her, you know,' said Gerald. 'Which is quite handy . . . saves petrol.'

Norman understood this convenience; his own marital infidelities had been with girls who lived out of the district. The back window of his car was constantly full of give-away gifts from petrol stations.

Greta got up from the table and went to the bar. She watched as Mr Patel removed the cellophane from a sausage roll and put the pink and brown object on a cardboard plate for Gerald to devour. She was going to *say* something, she didn't know what, or to whom, but she was going to manufacture a small drama out of this tense atmosphere between the small groups of men and women. Greta needed drama in her life, it was oxygen to her. Without it she slumped, pale and lifeless. She was a big woman who needed big events. She felt she was born to star in *La Traviata*, but always seemed fated to sing in the chorus of *The Gondoliers*. She picked on Norman Parker.

'I see your ex-wife has done all right for herself,' she said. 'Under-manager at Tesco's now, isn't she?'

Norman's face set hard, his toes curled inside his industrial boots. 'Must be hard up if they have to promote *her*,' he growled. He spun out drinking the last of his beer to give him time to think but nothing came to him. Gerald helped him out.

'Everybody knows how your wife got promotion,' he said.

'How did she?' asked Norman, who genuinely didn't know.

'On her back, of course,' said Gerald encouragingly, trying to catch Norman's eye, but Norman was looking away.

Greta ordered two vodkas and orange for herself and Maureen, and a port and lemon for Coventry. Mr Patel busied himself at the optics and tried to look inconspicuous. He thought, 'I would kill a man who insulted my wife, even my ex-wife, in such a fashion. I would chop him into small pieces and feed him to the large goldfish who swim in the ornamental pond in the foyer of the restaurant owned by my brother-in-law.'

Norman turned, grim-faced, and said, 'How do *you* know?'

Gerald laughed cynically and said, 'Norman, it's common know-ledge. She's not known as "The Grand Canyon" for nothing.'

Norman's knowledge of geography was not extensive but he sensed a terrible insult and hit Gerald Fox on his upper arm.

Mr Patel's finger was already dialling the first of three nines. Coventry rose to go but Greta pulled her down, saying, 'Finish your drink. Port doesn't grow on trees, you know.'

Coventry sat back and thought, 'Port *does* grow on trees . . . initially.'

Maureen, who was a wrestling fan, was shouting encouragement to Norman, who was pummelling Gerald around the shoulders. Gerald was trying to soothe Norman's pride (and save wear and tear on his suit) by saying: 'Only a joke Norman, only a joke.' But Norman's fist caught him a cruel blow on the side of his neck and made reasoning difficult. So Gerald was obliged to start fighting back. The men were well matched in build and weight and were still fighting when two spotty policemen came into the bar, carrying their peaked hats under their arms like rugby footballs.

Greta sat back in her seat, satisfied and happy. There was no blood, but the strong possibility of an arrest and a subsequent court case, with herself as star witness. She would wear her black and white hound's-tooth checked suit. It would contrast nicely with the dark panelling of the magistrates' court.

The spottier of the two policemen imposed himself between Gerald and Norman, who were both pleased that a higher authority had intervened and relieved them of the responsibility of ending the fight themselves. Coventry again got up to leave, but the less spotty policeman said: 'Sit down, madam, until this is sorted out.'

Coventry protested, 'But I'm not involved with either of them.'

Norman shouted, 'Oh yes you are, you lying cow . . . *you're Gerald Fox's mistress, and have been for the past year.*'

They haven't been mentioned earlier, being unimportant until now, but there were other people sitting in the Astaire's bar that night and all of them heard Norman's allegation clearly. Thirty per cent of them had problems and didn't retain the information. However, seventy per cent not only retained it but relished it and told other people. And so it became widely known on the Grey Paths Council Estate that Coventry Dakin and Gerald Fox were lovers and had been brawling in Astaire's and wasn't it awful and her with two children and a respectable husband and him with four lovely little girls and a wife who had a nervous disposition and couldn't watch horror films on the television.

Greta left the pub a disappointed woman. Mr Patel would not prefer charges, as he preferred no publicity. The young policemen lectured Norman and Gerald dispassionately. They used many obscenities to prove that they were men of the world, then left, after refusing Mr Patel's offer of free sausage rolls. They discussed Coventry Dakin in the police car and decided that Gerald Fox was a lucky man. Because of excessive overtime duties neither was experienced with women. They couldn't wait to be transferred to Vice.

3 I Leave the City of My Birth

I was halfway through cleaning my chimney on Wednesday afternoon when I ran across the road to my neighbour's house, opened the door, picked up the nearest object to hand, an Action Man doll, and brought its heavy little head hard down on the back of Gerald Fox's bulging neck.

Fox immediately stopped strangling his wife and fell down dead. Action Man's hinged torso swung for a few seconds and then was still. I let go of his feet and the little soldier fell onto the carpet and lay there in a theatrical attitude with both plastic hands raised in the air. A trickle of blood escaped from Gerald Fox's left ear.

My neighbour's children crept from behind a ragged sofa and attached themselves to their mother, and I let myself out of the house and started running. I was dressed in my chimney-sweeping clothes. I was covered in soot and I didn't have my handbag.

The first part of my escape route consisted of pedestrian pathways. I ran up and down ramps. I disappeared into the ground via subways. I grew bigger or smaller according to the size of the buildings. I was dwarfed by tower blocks and made gigantic by pensioners' bungalows. I hurried along past the boarded-up windows in the Bluebell Wood Shopping Mall. I went by St Osmond's, the concrete church with the stainless-steel spire, where I'd attended five ill-fated weddings. On towards Barn Owl Road, the main thoroughfare, which leads from the estate towards the city.

Halfway along this road I stopped to catch my breath. In an adjacent house a family were eating. Their living-room was lit up like Madison Square Gardens. There were five of them, dispersed around a three-piece suite. Each of them had a plate of steaming food on their laps. The pepper and salt and a ketchup bottle were balanced on the arms of the sofa. The television had their full attention. Nobody was speaking. They were chewing the cud. I wondered at their willingness to display such an intimate activity to casual passers-by.

Behind me, in my deserted kitchen, was a table laid with

Wednesday's table-cloth. Four places were set. A cruet stood exactly in the middle of the table. Four tubular chairs waited by each place setting. Daddy Bear, Mummy Bear, two teenage Bears. But Mummy Bear would not be at home tonight.

There is something heartbreaking about families. Such fragile blood ties. So easily snapped.

As I ran along the pavement beside the dual carriageway I thought I saw my husband looking down at me from the top deck of a rush-hour bus. But it may have been another middle-aged man with a gloomy expression wearing a hat too big for his head. I was now going against the tide of people who were returning from the city to the suburbs. Few people were going in my direction. For who needs to travel from the suburbs into the city at six o'clock in the evening? Apart from office cleaners and murderers escaping from outlying districts.

I ran because I am very frightened of policemen. As other people recoil from snakes or spiders and yet others refuse to travel in lifts or aeroplanes, so I avoid policemen. When I was a child I had black-and-white nightmares about Dixon of Dock Green. The sight of a lone officer of the law strolling along a sunlit street induces terror in me. I blame my parents for this irrational fear. (Though now, in my present circumstances, of course, my fear was entirely rational.)

I was now on the outskirts of the city. In the distance, coming nearer with each step, was the redbrick hospital where once I'd screamed and burst a blood vessel in my eye whilst giving birth to my son. Behind the tall chimney of the hospital incinerator was the converted hosiery factory, now a sixth-form college where the same son was studying for a better future.

I ran across the recreation ground where, years ago, I'd played on the swings while my own mother was enjoying herself in one of the many outpatients' clinics she frequented. 'It gets me out of the house,' she'd say, as she replaced her best underwear in the drawer until the next visit.

The smooth, wooden swing seats had been replaced by pastel plastic replicas. I sat down on a swing and tried to control my ragged breathing. Automatically I pushed my feet off the ground and began to work myself higher and higher. The night air streamed through my hair. I stood up on the seat and from my new vantage point I saw the railway station clock. I decided to catch a train, any train. The first that came in. I would go anywhere so long as it was *away*. Far away from the policemen investigating Gerald Fox's violent death.

I jumped off the swing and ran up the hill towards the station. On my way I passed buildings that were no longer there. An opera house where I'd seen Cinderella arrive at the ball in a twinkling coach, drawn by four Shetland ponies wearing plumed head-dresses. A hotel which had a basement bar with pink lights and was frequented by young men who powdered their noses and were served drinks by a barman who wore high heels. A tea-shop where old women sat and caught their breath and sorted their shopping bags before making for the bus. A pub called the White Swan where, as a child, I had felt drunk just sniffing the beery smell which escaped whenever the door opened. A baker's shop where the proprietor stood in the window icing tiered wedding cakes, proud of her skill and modestly accepting the compliments of the small crowd that always gathered outside on the pavement to watch. A pet shop where puppies frisked in too-small cages. A garage with two petrol pumps on the oil-stained pavements where, after rain, mad colours appeared for which no adult could ever give a logical explanation. The hardware shop where kettles and enamel mugs and calendars and a thousand more things were hung outside to chink and rattle in the slightest breeze. The drinking club where big men in loud suits used to emerge at four o'clock in the afternoon, wincing at the daylight.

All gone. Everything gone. Bulldozed. Flattened and taken away in lorries to a tip. And nobody tried to stop it because nobody knew the words or the procedure and anyway they were mesmerized by the word 'progress', which was given in explanation. A road was built in the place of the buildings. The same road raced around the city, slicing off the river and the parks, forcing the pedestrians underground into stinking subways where security cameras monitored their nervous progress.

I arrived at the top of the hill and stood opposite the station. I looked down on the little city. The spires of abandoned churches pricked the sky. To my left was a 'Sandwich Centre', to my right a 'Money Centre', behind me a 'Transport Centre'. All three signs were made of daglo orange plastic and had tipsy black letters. I turned and looked into the window of the 'Transport Centre'. A tired-looking man was sitting behind a counter, speaking into a radio microphone. A sign above him said in multi-coloured felt-tip:

Notice to Passengers
1. No fish and chips in taxis (Also no hot food)
2. No spitting in taxis
3. No fighting in taxis
4. No vomiting in taxis (Else pay £5
   and clean up mess, £10 at weekends)
5. After midnight £2 deposit to be paid
   to driver before commencing journey
6. You travel at your own risk!
7. Anyone leaving taxi without paying full fare
   will be found and *dealt* with

Rule number seven frightened me quite a lot because I was planning to evade my train fare by forcing myself through the ticket barrier if necessary. But when I arrived at the station I saw that the interior had been modernized. The ticket barrier had gone. British Rail had kindly removed this obstacle to my escape and the station now had an 'open policy'. Anyone could stroll in off the street and avail themselves of the facilities.

As I walked along the covered wooden bridge which spanned the railway lines and led to the various platforms, I heard an announcement that the eighteen twenty-three from Nottingham would shortly be arriving at platform three. The train would not be stopping until it reached London St Pancras. The first-class carriages were at the front of the train, the second-class carriages at the rear. And the buffet car was conveniently situated somewhere between the two.

Legitimate travellers came out of the Travellers Fare buffet on platform three, where a sign exhorted: 'Grabba Bacon Butty'. The train arrived and I got on it and stood in a corridor. I lied my way to London St Pancras via a sympathetic ticket collector.

'My husband is working in London. I've just had a telephone call to say that he's been crushed by a pile of bricks.'

By now I was sobbing genuine tears of shock. The ticket collector dabbed at my sooty face with a British Rail paper towel and said, 'Give me your address, love, and we'll say nowt else about it.' I lied through my tears and gave the address of the type of house I'd always wanted:

'The Hollyhocks'
Rose Briar Lane
Little Sleeping
Derbyshire

He wrote it down. Then he made his way to the buffet car and, following him, I heard snatches of his conversation. 'Lovely woman … husband crushed by bricks … intensive care … cleaning chimney.'

I stopped crying when a woman in an overall plonked a cardboard carton of sweet tea in front of me and said, 'Don't worry, love. My husband had a central heating pipe go through him once, but he plays snooker twice a week now.'

With or without the pipe? I wondered and laughed.

The woman looked nervously around the carriage and said, 'You'd better come in the kitchen.'

For the rest of the journey I sat on an upturned bread crate and sobbed while the buffet bar staff served, toasted, microwaved and bickered in the hot, confined space around me. To please them I swallowed two aspirins, washed down with a British Rail miniature of brandy.

It was dark when I stumbled and fell off the train at St Pancras Station. I lay on my back on the platform and saw my first dark London sky through the mottled glass of the high-spanning arched roof. Eager hands helped me to my feet but I didn't stop to thank them. I was off and running into London.

Right or left? Left. I ran down dirty steps. An illuminated sign ahead said: 'King's Cross'. I stood at a crossing. A traffic light ordered red buses and black taxis to stop for me. I crossed and went into the station. I needed to go to the lavatory urgently. I looked frantically for a sign; it was there. The friendly symbol of an armless woman in a triangular frock.

I ran down the steps towards a bad smell. A turnstile. A notice: 10p. I didn't have 10p. My bladder was bursting. A disgruntled black woman looked up from her knitting. She was the attendant. Her eyes slid over my dirty clothes, my black hands and face.

'Can you let me through, please? I must go to the toilet.'

'Ten pee,' the woman said. She didn't smile.

'I haven't got ten pee,' I said.

A queue had built up behind me. A little girl was crying. Her legs were slapped; she cried louder. I moved aside to let the irritable mother of the little girl through. This woman had two large suitcases, a shoulder-bag and a crying child to squeeze through the turnstile.

The attendant watched as the woman juggled her burdens. The backs of the little girl's legs were marked with her mother's palm-prints. The harassed mother passed through into the tiled paradise. Her little daughter's pathetic crying echoed and was then muffled, as a cubicle door was slammed shut.

I asked again, 'Please let me in.'

The attendant got to her feet. I sensed that rage was never far from her and it was present now. 'You go away, you bad woman. You can't get nothin' for nothin'. You gotta pay like all the people. I ain't havin' you in here with your meths and your drugs and your nastiness.'

She barred my way with her massive body. She was the Keeper of the Turnstile. The Controller of Bladders. The Director of Bowels. To enter her kingdom I needed a magical piece of silver.

'What can I do?' I asked her. 'Where can I go?'

'That's your problem,' she answered. 'S'your fault for livin' like you does.'

She thought I was a tramp. So did the women coming in and out of the turnstile. They were looking at my dirty clothes and skin. They avoided touching me with fastidious care. I went back up the steps to the station concourse. I saw other badly dressed dirty women; they had terrible teeth and flapping shoes. They were sitting on the floor passing a sherry bottle between them. There were three of them. I approached them and asked them for ten pence . . . 'for the toilet'.

'Now I ain't 'eard that one before,' said the eldest of the three.

'I'm desperate to go,' I said and danced a little jig on the marble floor.

'Go round the back, then,' said a purple-faced Scotswoman. 'Dinna waste money on pissin' and shittin'. Tha's just throwin' yer money away.'

'Round the back?'

The eldest got unsteadily to her feet. 'She means the hotel. Nip in the hotel . . . the Northern. Wait till the receptionist has turned her back and just nip in.'

'It's lovely in there,' said the youngest, wiping her mouth. 'I 'ad a wash in there last week. They've got flowered soap and a real towel. I did me feet 'fore I got chucked out.'

I now had to concentrate totally on keeping my bladder under control. I walked quickly round to the back of the station, past the lines of waiting taxis, until I saw the hotel. I hurried up the steps. I looked through the glass doors. Many people in uniforms were lounging around the reception desk. I could not wait. I walked through the doors and turned right. I saw a sign: 'GENTLEMEN'. I walked towards it. I heard a shout behind me, a young voice . . . female . . . 'Can I help you?'

I didn't look back. I pushed into the door marked 'GENTLEMEN'. The smell was like another, invisible, door to be pushed through. A young man was standing at the urinal; his eyes widened and he turned his body away when he saw me. He splashed his white shoes. 'Wrong place,' he said.

I crashed a cubicle door open . . . empty. I tore at my clothes and sat down. The relief was immediate, my body relaxed . . . I was floating. When every last drop was drained from my body I stood up and tucked my clothes about me. Glancing down, I saw a pair of white shoes at the bottom of the door. I stood very still, waiting for the shoes to move. Eventually the young man said: 'Are you coming out, then?'

I didn't speak. I didn't move. I waited. Water dripped, the smell intensified, I could hear his breath. He lit a cigarette. There was a commotion outside the door and a crowd of loud, masculine voices entered. White Shoes moved away.

'There's a woman in there,' he said excitedly.

There was rumbling laughter, then a knock on the cubicle door. 'Anybody there?'

I didn't speak. . . . Anything I said could only be ridiculous.

'Are you all right, love?' A Midlands accent like my own, but overlaid with drink and laughter. 'If you're feeling poorly, I'll come in there 'n help you. I've gorra cistificate for First Aid.'

His shoes were tightly laced, black and reassuring, with polished uppers and badly replaced soles and heels. When I didn't reply he spoke again. 'Come out and have a drink with us, duck.'

Another pair of shoes appeared at the bottom of the door. Grey, tasselled slip-ons. 'Come on, Arthur, there's no time for a drink. We'll miss the train. She's bound to be a slag anyway, in't she?'

Arthur said sadly, 'I've known some bleddy lovely slags in my time. First gel I went with wurra slag. You could 'ave a laugh with a slag.

24

You knew where you were in them days. Course it's different now – unless you've gorra condom on yer, even a slag don't wanna know yer. So, where does it leave yer? Yer *forced* to go to Soho and look for a pro. And *she* wants fifty quid for a bit o' light relief! How can *I* afford fifty quid? Who *can*, 'part from bleddy stockbrokers and suchlike? Bleddy London. You've gorra be a soddin' millionaire to live 'ere. Two pound a pint! Three pound fifty for a fry-up in a caff! An' the price of an 'otel room! Well, 's'no wonder folks're sleepin' on the bleddy pavements. I tell you, I wunt live in London if you stuck diamonds up me bum.'

White Shoes said: 'They're *all* slags . . . women, every bloody one of 'em, when it comes down to it . . . wherever they live.'

Arthur said, dangerously: '*My Wife Is A Woman*.'

White Shoes went on, oblivious to the threat in Arthur's voice, 'So was my ex-wife but *she* ran off, din't she? With a spade.'

'Keen gardener, was she?' said Arthur.

White Shoes continued, 'Your wife could be getting out of somebody's bed right now . . . as I'm speaking . . .'

But White Shoes spoke no more. It sounded as though his throat was being squeezed. I watched the assorted shoes scuffling about and listened to the parliamentary sound of men fighting. Then, when I judged that they had moved far enough away from my cubicle door, I flung it open and ran out of the lavatory. As I sped past them I got a quick impression of Arthur squeezing White Shoe's face into a gargoyle shape.

It was summer inside the hotel but outside it was a cold autumn. As I walked back towards the main road I began to feel self-conscious about my appearance. I have always dressed carefully, choosing clothes that played down my figure. With my looks I can't afford to wear anything too noticeable. My daughter Mary once said, 'You must be the only woman in the world who hasn't had her ears pierced.'

But I've always had a horror of being taken for a tart. Perhaps I went too far the other way: I have often been mistaken for a teacher in my plaid skirts, twin sets and flat shoes. I am a very methodical woman, which is why I keep a set of old clothes for when I sweep the chimney, once a year. These clothes were certainly not intended to be worn in London. I was wearing one of Derek's old Tortoise

Society sweatshirts, which was screen-printed with a picture of a smiling tortoise, a pair of pale blue polyester bell-bottom trousers and black plimsolls. I was covered in soot. My fingernails were black half moons. If I had seen myself coming I would have crossed the road to avoid me. I wanted to turn myself inside out, like a reversible jumper I once had. I was painfully cold. Icy draughts blew up the sleeves and down the neck of my baggy sweatshirt and played around my chest and back. I moaned with each gust of wind and there was no reaching for a warm sweater, no coat hanging on the back of the door, no fire to crouch in front of when I got home. I had no home.

I hope you'll believe that normally I am a fastidiously clean woman. I bathe every day, which is considered eccentric behaviour amongst my friends and relations. Ordinarily I would never leave the house without first cleaning my fingernails and making sure that my anorak hood was straight. So my instinct now was to keep my filthy self hidden away in the dark. But darkness is cold, so once again I was pulled towards the illusion of warmth given by the lights of King's Cross Station.

The three women were still sitting on the floor. They were now singing a maudlin Irish song, something about a lovelorn butcher boy who hanged himself on his wedding day. I would have liked to join them and ask if they'd got a spare coat I could borrow; but I knew that their singing would soon attract the attention of the authorities. In the city where I lived I have often seen buskers bullied away from shop doorways by policemen; once, even, a violinist playing Mozart, the height of musical respectability. So I kept away from the group and walked around the station looking for dropped coins.

Envy is a destructive emotion but I envied everyone I saw that night. I envied them their coats, sweaters, shoes, boots, handbags, money, chips, cups of tea, clean skin and clear consciences. I envied them the beds they would sleep in, the front doors they would open, the cigarettes they would smoke. I've never had time for people such as my husband, who constantly indulge themselves in self-pity. But I have to confess that, as I stood and watched the people purposefully walking about the station, I felt very sorry for myself indeed.

It was now eleven o'clock. Drunks in dinner jackets joined the queues for the trains. A pretty girl met a pretty man off a train from Scotland. They said 'I love you' to each other. The girl was more enthusiastic than the man. An old woman with a shaking disease pulled a too-heavy suitcase towards the taxi rank. A skinhead with a spider tattooed on his neck ran athletically for a train and caught it, leaving shock waves of public alarm behind him. 'Only muggers run,' said a man to his wife.

The automatic doors opened and a pair of policemen walked through. I stood behind a pillar and watched them stop the song about the suicidal Irish butcher. The three chaotic women stood up unsteadily and fussed over their slithering mountain of plastic bags. Eventually they moved on and out into the wet night. The policemen watched them go, then they strolled around the station, looking for minor infringements of the law.

I, who had infringed the law in the most major way possible, moved around the station to avoid them. Blue lights flashed outside and more policemen poured through the entrances. Some of them were trying to control wild-eyed Alsatian dogs which were straining on short choke chains. They looked as though they hated humanity and constantly lurched towards innocent passers-by, barking. One dog, called Baskerville by his handler, was in such a frenzy that it had to be choked into silence, watched, at a distance, by censorious British animal lovers. There was an announcement on the loudspeakers: 'The nine-thirty football special from Leeds has now arrived. Members of the public are asked to keep clear and assist the police in their duties. British Rail apologizes to members of the *bona fide* public for any inconvenience they may suffer as a result of football fans passing through this station.'

Hidden behind a pile of luggage I could see the train as it pulled in with its cargo of young men. They were waving red and white scarves out of the carriage windows. They were singing, ''Ere we go, 'ere we go, 'ere we go.' The sound crackled around the station. There was enough electric power in their combined voices to run a fleet of milk floats. As the train stopped, the policemen ran and stood two to each carriage door. The Alsatians seemed not to like the colours red and white; they leapt at the open carriage windows, as if their teeth were aching for football supporters' flesh. Baskerville was head-butting the carriage in frustrated frenzy. All down the train, carriage windows were slammed shut. The singing stopped. The dogs were out of control. The *bona fide* public corralled themselves into corners of the station, away from the dog handlers who strained and shouted, 'Sit! Sit!' and choked the dogs into uneasy submission. Baskerville was the last to quieten down; his eyes were rolling around in his crazy head. He yipped and yapped and scooted his powerful haunches along the platform towards the train. He *was* sitting, but only just.

A police inspector ordered the carriage doors to be opened. Then he spoke through a mechanized loud hailer to the young men. 'Once on the platform you must line up in fours, and wait until everyone is off the train. You will then be escorted from the station to the Underground. Anyone trying to leave the station unescorted will be arrested and charged with . . .' The inspector broke off, a note of uncertainty had crept into his voice.

A foolhardy youth wearing a primrose-coloured sweater shouted, 'Charged wiv what . . . ?' Baskerville was brought through the crowd to answer the youth's question. When everyone was assembled on the platform and the train had been checked for damage, the youths, dogs and policemen began their sullen procession.

A youth said, 'I don't wanna go on the Underground. I only live round the corner.' A policeman pushed him back into the ranks.

Where have I seen a similar sight? I think hard and remember. It was *All Our Yesterdays* on television. People from the ghetto were being rounded up and taken somewhere. A policeman is looking at me from across the concourse. I blush under my soot, look at my non-existent watch, remember an appointment and walk out of the station and back into London.

Outside there is a little hut full of newspapers and pornographic magazines. I look at the headlines: 'HOMELESS – NEW SHOCK'. I riffle quickly through the pages. Nothing about me murdering a man earlier in the day. The newspaper seller says, 'If you ain't buyin' get your dirty hands off that paper.' I say I am sorry and cross the road with a crowd of other people, grateful for the accidental shelter of their umbrellas. The rain is dark and spiky; within a few minutes I am saturated. Bubbles froth along the rubber edging of my plimsolls. There is no point in trying to avoid the puddles, so I walk through them. I don't know what to do with my hands. There they are, jiggling away at my sides, carrying nothing, holding nothing, pushing nothing. I try crossing my arms but it feels wrong, all right for standing at my back door and taking the night air, but out of place in London in the rain after midnight. Hands on hips? . . . No . . . too suggestive. Hands behind back? . . . Ludicrous . . . looks like I'm being satirical about the Royal Family. So I let them hang down and after a while I forget them and am comfortable. This is how men walk.

A sign tells me that I'm in the London Borough of Camden, a place I've never heard of. I look around and on the opposite side of the road I see a storybook castle with turrets and spires and many-arched windows. Is it Westminster Abbey? Is the River Thames around the next corner? Then I see a sign on the beautiful building says: 'St Pancras Station' and I feel foolish. Is Buckingham Palace nearby? Where is Piccadilly Circus? I think about my children. How will they cope when they find out their mother is a murderess? I want an anorak, a cigarette, a cup of tea, an umbrella, a bar of soap and a chair. I walk on. The buildings are swirling over my head. I cannot encompass them; they are too many, they are too high. They are built of yellow, dirty brick, when I am used to red brick. They are not friendly buildings, they are too important: headquarters and official residences, and further on shops with impossible, unthinkable prices.

I am frightened of London, I want to go home. My feet are numb, I don't know where to go, or which street to turn down. I want to rewind my life on a video machine and wake up yesterday morning. I can't cry; my heart is frozen inside me. There is no question of giving myself up to the police. What I have done is wicked and I shall be punished; but I shall punish myself. There is no need for the law to intervene in what is now a private matter.

4 Excitement in Badger's Copse Close

Greta was standing at the stove, stirring tinned rice pudding, when Maureen crashed through the kitchen door; coming from darkness into sudden fluorescent light.

'Coventry has killed Gerald Fox!'

'*Coventry?*'

'Yes!'

'*Killed?*'

'Yes!'

'*Gerald Fox?*'

'YES!'

'*Coventry has killed Gerald Fox?*'

'YES!'

An explosion of enjoyment filled the kitchen. The two women, trembling and shocked, but also excited and happy, began to talk. Coventry's life was examined for previous displays of aggression. Greta remembered the time that Coventry had spoken to her sharply once.

Greta had remarked that Derek didn't deserve Coventry who, in Greta's opinion, was younger, better-looking, nicer and far more interesting and intelligent than Derek.

Coventry had replied, very irritably, that Derek had married her when she was an ignorant teenager who was in and out of work, living in her parents' house and having to obey her parents' rules. Derek, however, was twenty-six, well established, in a job with prospects and already had his name on the council house waiting list.

To this, Greta said, 'Big deal!' Coventry had run out of Greta's house and slammed the front door. Disappointing, in that it lacked drama perhaps, but worth two minutes in the telling. The two women felt important and were conscious of their high status in these dramatic events; after all, they were Coventry's best friends.

They moved into the living-room and watched as official vehicles came to a halt outside the Foxes' house. Greta did a count: three ambulances; five police cars; one white police van; a fire engine (had

30

Coventry turned to arson as well?); three plain cars carrying six plain men; and a rocky little Citroën containing one gaudily dressed social worker. The street had seen nothing like it since a wedding reception had turned nasty and temporarily stopped the traffic while the men of both families slogged it out. Greta and Maureen went outside and joined the throng of neighbours standing behind the plastic ribbon of the police barricade. Every now and again all the heads turned to look at the Dakins's house, where the murderess's husband was expected home from work.

5 I Meet Mr Periwinkle

It is two o'clock in the morning. I am sitting outside the London Foot Hospital in a place called Fitzroy Square. I can't walk another step, but the rain has stopped and my clothes have dried on me. I am grateful for such small mercies. To my delight I found three strong elastic bands inside the doorway. One I used to fasten my damp hair into a pony-tail, the other two I used to wrap around the superfluous folds of flapping cloth at my ankles. Bell-bottoms were the ultimate extreme of flares. I have only worn them once outside the house before and then a high wind blew up and billowed the surplus cloth. From the knees down I looked like a galleon in full sail. Derek was pleased when they were relegated to chimney-sweeping wear. He hates unconventional clothing. It unsettles him.

Before I went to sleep I wiped my hands and face with wet leaves from the square. I was desperate to get rid of the soot. Two nurses swaddled in warm cloaks passed me. They looked on curiously as I scrunched the leaves over my face. As they walked past me I heard one say, '*I* like the smell of autumn leaves as much as anybody, but sticking them up your nose is going too far.' The other said, 'That reminds me, I'm starting my psychiatric training next month.'

The wet leaves made no impression on the soot. Looking in a lamplit puddle I saw a dusky face staring back at me. I was reminded of the Black and White Minstrels, their horrible winking and grimacing and strutting around with canes and top hats. They were a firm favourite of Derek's. He wrote to the BBC when the show was taken off. I remember one phrase in his letter, 'Clean family entertainment.' He signed himself: 'Derek A. Dakin'.

My head lolls forward; am I asleep? I don't know, hard to tell, my brain is tired. My eyes drop shut. . . . The sun is shining. I am warm. An old man with mutton-chop whiskers and kindly eyes is holding out his hands. 'Come, my dear,' he says. He pulls me to my feet. 'I'm Mr Periwinkle,' he says. 'Breakfast is ready.' He crosses the square and indicates that I am to follow him. We stop outside a tall house. 'I live here with my invalid daughter, Emily,' the old man explains. The front door is opened by Les Dawson wearing a pantomime cook's costume. Les smirks as I squeeze by him in the narrow hall. Mr Periwinkle shows me into a room at the back of the house. Sunshine floods in, bleaching the colours of the furniture and decorations. Mr Periwinkle says, 'Emily, we have a guest for breakfast.'

I hadn't noticed the wheelchair in the corner or its occupant. Emily wheels herself towards me. Her little face is pale under her lace cap and brown ringlets. She lisps, 'I saw you sleeping in the doorway last night. Were you dweadfully cold?'

I answer, 'Upon my life I was most fearfully cold, Miss Periwinkle.'

'I told Papa as soon as I was dwessed, didn't I, Pa? I said, "It is our Cwistian duty to help that poor unfortunate. You must get weady at once and invite her to share our bweakfast." Didn't I, Papa?'

Mr Periwinkle kisses the tips of his daughter's white fingers. 'My little gal has not long to live,' he confesses in an undertone. 'But ain't she just the most perfect angel you ever saw?'

Les Dawson brings in every breakfast food I'd ever heard of. I gorge myself on porridge and boiled eggs and toast and kidneys and kedgeree and bacon and sausages. I eat six slices of toast and drink five cups of scalding coffee. Emily nibbles on an arrowroot biscuit and sips on a thimble-sized cup of warm milk. Mr Periwinkle's eyes twinkle at the end of the table as he watches me eat. Then he gets up and pokes the fire and invites me to sit by the hearth and tell my story. When I am seated opposite him I say, 'There are two things you should know about me immediately. The first is that I am beautiful.'

'Indeed you are, ma'am.'

'The second is that yesterday I killed a man called Gerald Fox.'

'Are you informing me that you are a murderer?' says Mr Periwinkle, whose eyes have stopped twinkling. 'In that case, Dawson, throw her out!'

As I am falling down the steps Les Dawson's face looms over me. He is saying something about his mother-in-law. . . .

It was getting light. A dustbin lorry was making its way around the square. Birds were flapping about in group panic; time to start walking. The dustbin lorry ground up. Two men walked briskly to the pile of black rubbish bags next to me. They both wore gloves and orange overalls. One was wearing horn-rimmed spectacles, the other a Russian fur hat. Spectacles shouted, 'You'll have to move, so's we can get to them bags, lady.'

Russian Hat bellowed, 'We've left you till last. Normally we *start* at the Foot Hospital. S'unusual for us to finish 'ere, ain't it, Spog?'

Spog adjusted his glasses and said, 'Un'eardov. But we could see you needed your sleep.'

I said, 'I've got cramp in both legs, I can't move yet.'

'I ain't surprised,' Spog shouted over the grinding mechanism of the lorry. 'Stuck in a bleedin' doorway all night. 'S a wonder you ain't been interfered wiv' an' all. Some blokes ain't fussy, you know. They'll go with anyfing, even dossers.'

'Can you help me up?' I asked.

'No we can't,' said Russian Hat. 'We ain't allowed to touch the public; 'specially women, case they go complainin' to somebody.'

The driver got out of the cab, a fat man with an Elvis Presley haircut and a string tie. He walked over to us with a showbiz swagger, as though he were appearing twice nightly at Caesar's Palace. His voice was flat and hard. 'Get out the way,' he ordered. I was frightened of him. So were Spog and his mate. I tipped onto my side and pulled myself onto the pavement. My dead legs trailed behind me. Fat Man picked the rubbish bags up with one hand and slung them into the back of the lorry. He nodded the other two men back to work, then came back to where I was lying, rubbing my legs and feet back to life. He spoke from lips that looked like two pink slugs.

'If I was Prime Minister, I'd pass a law that gave the Council the right to throw you, an' your sort, into the back of my lorry. *You're rubbish*. I'd have the dossers, the winos, the dope 'eads, the whores, the glue sniffers, the pakis, the chinks, the darkies, the whole bleedin' lot of you pulled to bits. Bones broke, heads off, mixed up by the mincer at the back of my motor. An' you know what? I'd work for nothin', 'cos I'd be doin' it for my country. You're rubbish! Fuck off out of it!'

I got up and hobbled away from him into a street leading from the square. As I regained the feeling in my feet and legs, I walked faster, until finally I was running along the empty pavement. Passing somewhere called Charlotte Street, where the restaurant and café windows were being cleaned by young men in denims, I could smell coffee, real coffee, the sort that people make in little machines after grinding beans. I have never tasted real coffee. When rare visitors

34

came to our house I didn't say, like actors do in television plays, 'It's only instant, I'm afraid.' In our house it was never anything but Maxwell House.

I enjoyed running, so I carried on, flying into a big street called Tottenham Court Road, past shops full of Japanese electrical goods. A golden sun rose on my right. My reflection flashed from shop windows as I ran, effortlessly and with increasing speed, dodging and weaving through people on the pavements. I now had something to do in London; I was an early-morning runner. Carry on, faster, faster, pony-tail bobbing, arms carving through the air, legs striding. Stop. I have arrived at the end of Tottenham Court Road. I have been here before. The street is called Euston Road. A shimmering angled building stands opposite. I passed it last night. A magical mirrored building, reflecting life and movement. I have come a full circle. St Pancras ... Fitzroy Square ... Tottenham Court Road. I have a territory.

The pavement is suddenly crowded. I wonder if there has been an accident but the crowd exists only for a moment and then disperses. People are coming out of an Underground station. They have the numb, hurrying look of people going to work. Chinese men with brief-cases, Arabs in flowing robes. An African woman, with tribal markings on her face and a squash of chiffon on her head, is holding her daughter's hand. The girl is wearing a miniature school uniform. I am captivated by the sight of so many different nationalities. Although I stand and watch the Underground travellers emerge for at least five minutes, I am disappointed not to see a single bowler hat. However, a policeman's helmet is visible through the crowd so, scared, I move on, running back in the direction I've come from.

A few cafés are open now. I'm so hungry that I can smell them before I see them. It would be very ill-mannered to stop and stare through the windows and watch people eating and drinking, so I pass by at speed. The traffic fills four lanes and moves in irritated fits and starts. It must be the famous London rush-hour. A Japanese tele-vision in a shop window is showing *TV AM*. The correct time is superimposed on Roy Hattersley's feet: 7.35 a.m. John and Mary will be getting up for school and college. No, they won't be going anywhere this morning. Today is the first full day of their new status. They are the children of a murderer. Opposite them live a widow and her four children.

I have created chaos in the dull street where I lived meekly for twenty-one years. I know I can never go back.

6 Inspector Sly Investigates

6.15 p.m. 13 Badger's Copse Close, Grey Paths Estate.
Wednesday evening.

Detective Inspector Sly was getting impatient. He hated slobbergobs and Derek Dakin had been talking for ten minutes and forty seconds non-stop. Sly took this opportunity to study Derek and the interior of the living-room. He made mental notes, later to be inscribed into his notebook.

1. Furnishings and carpets: beige (also curtains)
2. Wallpaper: beige (with cherry pattern)
3. Framed pictures of steam trains (seven)
4. Bookcase: box files, encyclopedias, tortoise reference books
5. Ornaments: few; tortoise trophies on TV, plus cup for third-year hurdles: winner, Coventry Lambert
6. Arrangement of dried grasses on small table
7. Pets: cats (two); one with conjunctivitis
8. Children: (two); boy and girl (clean types)
9. Husband: (one) boring fart
10. Proof that Coventry Dakin has been domiciled at this address: pair of fluffy mules (size 6½) by the fireside
11. Wedding photo on bookcase: bride beautiful, smiling; groom rat-faced, unsmiling
12. Brown plastic handbag, containing: child benefit book, hairbrush, pkt clothes pegs, keys, bus tickets, two tampons (regular size), one cat's flea-collar

Sly broke into Derek's consciousness by raising his voice and looking stern. 'So what time was it when you last saw your wife, Mr Dakin?'

Derek started to whimper and examine his fingernails; tears gathered in his eyes. Sly mentally noted:

13. Husband: possible poofter?

37

Coventry's children left the room. They had never seen their father display extreme emotion before. The sight of Derek's distorted face, together with the undignified grunts heaving from his chest, drove them into the hall. Sly shouted after them, 'Don't leave the house, I shall need to talk to you next.' Detective Inspector Sly offered Derek no comfort; in his experience it only started them off again. Nor did he loan his handkerchief; he never got them back.

'It was the word "wife" that set me off,' Derek explained to Sly, as soon as he had stopped gulping and sobbing. 'A wife is a woman who wears an apron and has her arms inside a mixing bowl. A wife is gentle and kind, and speaks loving words to her family. A wife doesn't murder her neighbour, and then run away from home. . . .'

Mary and John Dakin sat at the bottom of the stairs. They looked like the non-threatening type of teenagers to be found inside the pages of a Littlewoods catalogue, usually pictured lounging on bales of hay, or beaming ecstatically on clean motorbikes. They didn't know what to think; nothing in their previous experience had prepared them for the shock of being told that their mother was a murderer. Neither of them knew what to say to each other. They listened to the rumble of voices behind the living-room door in silence. The door opened; Detective Inspector Sly stood there, imposing in his dark uniform. 'Mary, be a good girl and make your dad a cup of tea . . . plenty of sugar . . . he's in shock.' Mary glanced into the living-room on her way to the kitchen. Derek was shaking his body about; saliva hung from his mouth; his fingers twisted together like mating snakes.

'My mother's a murderer, and my father's gone mad,' thought Mary. She conjured up the atmosphere in the house at breakfast-time that morning. It was normal . . . ordinary . . . average . . . conventional. It was dull . . . safe . . . nice . . . there was NOTHING TO WORRY ABOUT. John stared down at the hall carpet; he was thinking that now he could never go back to sixth-form college where he was doing A levels. Not unless he dyed his hair and took to wearing sunglasses during the day. Worse, *Coventry*, his mother's stupid name, would be in the papers. He had told his friends at college that her name was Margaret.

Inspector Sly stood up; the interview with Derek was nearly over. Derek was howling like an upset wolf. Sly watched him contemptuously. He thought, 'Give me five minutes alone with him in the cells and I'd make a man of him. A good kicking is what he needs.' Detective Inspector Sly was an inveterate advocate of a good kicking. He'd seen it work wonders. Men had left the police station with their backs invisibly bruised but their heads held high.

Mary came into the room with two mugs of thin, milky tea. She averted her eyes from her father. Sly gave her one of his 'strong man with heart of gold' glances; this consisted of slightly inclining his head, while pursing his lips and twinkling his eyes. 'I can see that you'll be a great comfort to your father in the days ahead, Mary,' said Sly, using his 'I know how to talk to teenagers' voice.

Derek burst into a loud crying fit again and Mary quickly left the room. She was repelled and disgusted by the snot and tears running down her father's face. She felt sorry for him, but sorrier for herself. Her life was ruined; she could never leave the house again. She would lose all her friends and now, with her mother gone, she would have to do all the ironing and housework. She looked at herself in the hall mirror. She thought: 'I've aged ten years, I look at least twenty-six.' She sucked on her gold necklace and sat back on the stairs, waiting to be called for her interrogation.

John was now upstairs, watching as Gerald Fox's body, after being photographed, prodded, fingerprinted and measured, was being finally loaded into the back of an ambulance. The enormity of his mother's crime struck John properly for the first time. Gerald Fox no longer existed. He was a husk, a nothing, a nuisance. John wondered about his own death. He thought he would prefer to die in his sleep, at the age of eighty-five or before he became incontinent, whichever came first. John looked at his mother's clothes hanging in her wardrobe. They were sensible and dull. Her shoes were worse. He opened the top drawer of her bedside cabinet and saw a packet of 'Handie-Andies' and five pairs of white cotton knickers. Then he found a locked diary hidden inside a hot water bottle cover. John put the diary inside his shirt. He didn't want Inspector Sly reading whatever his mother had written. The gilt lock felt cold against his chest. He quietly searched the room for the key but found nothing. He would wait until this awful night was over and his father and Mary were asleep, and then he would break into the diary and read his mother's thoughts. As he closed the door he whimpered under his breath, 'Oh Mum, Mum.'

Inspector Sly had found the video tape of *Vile Bodies*. He was holding it out to Derek, who was denying ever having seen it before. Mary was shaking her head. Inspector Sly said, 'It must be the lad's, then.' John came into the room and put Inspector Sly straight. No, he'd never seen it before; he wasn't into that sort of thing. Pornography was boring and demeaned women. Sly thought, 'Sanctimonious little git.' He said, 'Well if it doesn't belong to anybody here, it must belong to *Mrs* Dakin.'

John and Mary glanced at each other and decided to say nothing in defence of their mother. After all, she wasn't here, but they were.

Derek blustered: 'My wife wouldn't allow that filth in the house, she wouldn't watch *The Benny Hill Show* without a cushion over her face. She's a lady.'

'Yes, a *lady killer*, Mr Dakin,' said Sly, pleased with the pun. 'Let me tell you something, old cock. None of us knows each other. We live cheek by jowl for years. We congratulate ourselves on knowing our spouses, inside and out. And then one day it's brought to our attention that we don't know one iota about what they're really like; happens all the time. My own wife, who's failed five driving tests out of nervousness, did a parachute jump for charity last week.'

7 Nelson and Trafalgar

Centre Point. I've heard of this building. It used to be famous. It looks empty and rigid. It's surrounded by a wind which drags and pushes people around its concrete walls. *I* would like to be inside Centre Point, in a room on my own at the very top of the building looking down, because I don't know where London begins or ends. Can I walk round it in a day, or would it take a week or a month?

As I walk down the Charing Cross Road I see two young men in business suits kissing. One jumps onto a slow-moving bus. The man remaining on the pavement continues to blow kisses until the bus is out of sight. I see a middle-aged woman, dressed immaculately in black and red. She catches the high heel of one shoe in a crack in the pavement. She stumbles and shouts, 'Oh bollocks!' She pulls the shoe out of the crack and looks despairingly at the torn suede. I see an old man, dressed in a trilby hat, ragged clothes and wellingtons, as he takes a saxophone out of a distressed case and starts to play 'Blue Moon'. A Japanese tourist takes the musician's photograph, stops to listen and applauds at the end of the number. He then requests 'Stars Fell on Alabama'. The saxophonist sways inside his wellingtons and goes into a routine, lifting his instrument, then lowering it, then inclining it from side to side. I can imagine him twenty-five years ago. I think that he wore a spangled tuxedo and played with a big band and never thought that he would get old. . . .

The Japanese tourist claps his hands and smiles and bows, but walks away without dropping money into the open case. 'I wish I could give you something,' I say to the old man, who is trying to catch his breath. 'You're very good.'

'No, I'm not *good*,' he says, wiping his cloudy eyes with the end of his check-patterned tie. 'I'm a very wicked man. God is aware of my many sins and is punishing me. I'm in hell. This is hell,' he says, indicating the exterior of a bookshop and half of the Charing Cross Road. 'I'm an object of pity, I have lost my dignity.'

I say, 'No, I meant that your playing is good.'

'My musical abilities have deteriorated considerably. I have painful arthritis in my fingers. God gave me the arthritis to remind me of my many sins. I can't afford the aspirins for the pain,' he adds. He puts out his hand; he is wearing a copper bracelet on his scrawny wrist.

'I haven't got anything,' I repeat. 'Not one penny.'

'Then go away,' he says. 'You are distracting me from my work. Aspirins are seventy-nine pence a packet.' As I walk away he begins to play 'As Time Goes By'.

I've always loved books. I'm passionate about them. I think books are sexy. They are smooth and solid and contain delightful surprises. They *smell* good. They fit into a handbag and can be carried around and opened at will. They don't change. They are what they are and nothing else. One day I want to own a lot of books and have them near to me in my house, so that I can stroll to my bookshelves and choose what I fancy. I want a harem. I shall keep my favourites by my bed.

The Charing Cross Road is a celebration to books: they are everywhere, lolling about in piles. Displaying themselves in windows. Artistically arranged in pyramids. Fanned on tables. Thrown into boxes. Stacked to ceiling height and heaped on floors. As I look into the shops my mouth waters and my fingers itch. I want to handle the books, caress them, open and devour them.

A party of foreign schoolchildren passed me; they were carrying plastic bags. Most of them were eating. One boy was wearing a plastic policeman's helmet. The elastic keeping the helmet in place was cutting into his chin.

As I watched, one of the children threw a paper-wrapped half-eaten hot dog into the gutter. If I'd been quicker I could have retrieved it and stuffed it into my mouth but I hesitated and a taxi squashed the hot dog and drove away with the remains stuck onto its front wheel.

I followed the children, hoping for more crumbs from their table. To my surprise, Trafalgar Square was at the bottom of the Charing Cross Road. The fountains frothed and sparkled in the sunshine. The foreign schoolchildren ran about with bags of birdseed, encouraging the pigeons to swoop down and feed, but when the birds enveloped them in a flapping mass, they screamed and waved their arms and sent the pigeons flying. A fat woman in a beige raincoat with a pixie hood was standing at the base of a metal lion, throwing pieces

42

of stale bread and cakes onto the floor in front of her. Fragments of iced fancies, toasted teacakes, scones and granary baps scattered around my feet. The woman crooned to the birds. 'Yes, my darlings, eat it all up, you'll be big and strong. Now, now! No squabbling! Stop it, you naughty boy!'

She was addressing her remarks to a scruffy brown bird that had landed on her shoulder. I wanted to run into the feathery mass and snatch the crumbs off the floor; and I was preparing to do just that when another large gang wheeled out of the sky and obliterated the food. The woman stooped amongst them emptying the bag. The pigeons covered her; their claws clung to her permed curls; she was laughing and protesting. 'Silly birds, get off at once, you're hurting me.'

But the birds continued to sit smugly on their human monument. When they eventually flew off the woman looked up and followed their flight path longingly. Then, earthbound and clumsy, she picked up the carrier bag, took a tissue from it and tried to wipe the pigeon excrement off her coat.

I said, 'They've ruined your coat.'

'No,' she said. 'It goes in the machine on a hot wash cycle and comes out as fresh as a new-minted sixpence. I come here every day so I *must* have a reliable washing machine. A Zanussi. It's the only one. I can fully recommend it. It's the only one that can cope with the pigeons' little presents. Goodbye.'

She picked her way daintily through the birds with many apologies: 'Sorry to disturb you, dears. May I pass by, birdies?'

I watched her as she reached the pavement, then lost sight of her in the crowds. I sat on the side of a fountain and tried to formulate a plan. I've always planned my life in advance. I'm a great believer in lists.

Yesterday's list was:

Order smokeless fuel
Clean chimney
Flea powder for Softy
Wash loose covers
Buy teen bra (34A cup)
Shave legs, pluck eyebrows
Pick Derek's tortoise book up from library

Find odd socks
Phone Mum about Sunday dinner
Post Noreen's birthday card
Has Bella got my big whisk?
Ask doctor if I'm going mad
Light bulbs
Christmas wrapping paper
Cancel the *Sun*
Find Derek's bicycle clip
Tackle Big Mouth about rumour

Today's list is:

Give myself up to the police?
Suicide?
Try to live in London?

I attempted to wash the soot away by using the water in the fountain but, even as I rubbed roughly at my skin, I knew that only hot water and a soapy lather would do the job.

I felt safe in Trafalgar Square; there were plenty of people about and they provided distraction from the cold and hunger and unhappiness I was feeling. In the afternoon a small crowd of demonstrators gathered to protest about something to do with South Africa. Somebody, Nelson Mandela, was in prison and the people in the square thought it was time he was let out. They crossed over the road and I went with them to the steps of a church. I stood in the most dense part of the crowd, to get warm and hide from the many police in attendance. A microphone couldn't be made to work, so an ancient man wearing a green duffel-coat formed a megaphone with his hands and shouted towards the people watching him. The wind and the noise of the traffic blew his voice away. Only a few words reached us: '. . . oppression . . . imperialist past . . . shame . . . racists . . . Thatcher . . . Reagan . . . God . . .'

A youth standing next to me said, 'Stupid ol' git, 'stime 'e wuz put down.' He scowled up at the old man in green.

'Why?'

''Cos he's past it, tha's why. He's bleedin' *old*; 'e's 'undred nex' week. 'Sno good *talkin'* 'bout gettin' Mandela outa prison; we gotta *do somethin'*. *Spring* 'im out, wiv an 'elicopter an' grenades an' stuff. I'd volunteer. I've never bin abroad,' he added.

A younger, vigorous man with a louder voice had replaced the old man, who was now being helped to sit on a camp-chair by a girl with a bald head.

'Comrades, our first speaker, Mortlake Greenfield, will be *one hundred years old* next week. So let's sing "For He's a Jolly Good Fellow" for the Grand Old Man of the Left.'

'Whad I tell ya?' said the youth triumphantly. '*'Undred!* Woz 'e know 'bout anythink? Grand Old Man of the Left,' he repeated contemptuously. 'If he was any *good* he'd be *dead*, wouldn't 'e? 'E'd 'ave *died*, fighting for a cause.'

I didn't join in the singing. My mouth was too dry, and 'For He's a Jolly Good Fellow' is a song I've always particularly hated.

At the end of the many passionate speeches I began to feel that poor Nelson Mandela should be let out of prison immediately. I joined in, shouting 'Free Nelson Mandela!' I even raised my arm in the air, although I didn't form a fist, like many of those around me were doing. When the crowd dispersed I felt colder and hungrier. I was now more concerned with myself than Nelson Mandela. I crossed over the road and walked quickly around the square to get warm. The bald girl I'd seen earlier came up to me and said, 'Are you aware, sister, that your pathetic attempt to empathize with black people by blackening your face is deeply insulting and patronizing to them?'

I said, 'It's soot.'

'Yes,' she said. 'Some people call them "sooties".'

'But I don't.'

'What do *you* call them?' she said with a smirk. Her friends were gathering round. Some were taking photographs.

'I call them whatever their names are,' I said.

'What do you call them *collectively*, though?'

'I don't call them anything any more,' I said. 'Everything seems to be insulting. If you'd give me a piece of soap and tell me where I can use free hot water, I'll wash the soot off. I'm sick of walking round with a dirty face.'

'Yeah. Can't take it, can you, sister? Well now you know what it's like to live in a racist society.'

A Rastafarian with spiky dreadlocks laughed loudly and said, 'Oh c'mon, Baldy. How do *you* know what it's like? You're as white as a bedsheet soaked in Persil yourself. Or ain't you looked in the mirror lately?' The girl's bald head flushed red.

'You're too tolerant, Kenroy,' she said. 'I'm pissed off with fighting your battles for you.'

Kenroy's grin slipped away. 'Listen darlin', I been meanin' to tell you. I like my women to have hair on their heads. I'm tired of wakin' up in the mornin' next to a *skull*. If it was a skull I wanted to look at, I could take myself to the British Museum.' The little crowd of onlookers drew in their breath. Kenroy sucked on his lips and shouted: 'Ta ta Baldy, I'll be round later to pick up me Sony and me socks.' The girl ran after him and he turned and they embraced, he stroking her bald head fondly, she kissing his neck.

I thought it was time to move away from the square and the unpleasantness that I seemed to be causing, but I didn't know where to go. It was nearly dark; the traffic raced around the edges of the square, like Red Indians encircling a closed-up wagon train.

I could have wept with the cold. I tried to find shelter from the wind at the base of a lion. If there had been room I would have curled up in between its metal paws. I wanted to be *in* something, something smaller than a public square.

I tried to remember films I'd seen about deprivation – people afloat at sea for weeks, or captured in prison camps. The survivors seemed to sing quite a lot, until their tongues got too swollen. I tried it; under my breath I sang:

> All I want is a room somewhere,
> Far away from the cold night air.
> With one enormous chair,
> Oh, wouldn't it be loverly?

I stopped when a young couple came and stood near to me. The girl was almost pretty. She was wearing a blue hat with a veil; her blue suit was wrinkled and too thin for October. She was shivering. Bits of confetti blew off her hair in the wind. The young man walked unsteadily; he pulled constantly at the too-tight collar of his white shirt. He had a red, angry-looking face. Somebody had recently given him a brutal haircut. He wore a drooping pink carnation in the buttonhole of his grey suit. He said, 'Well, you've seen the fountains, can we get back to the hotel now?'

She said, 'Oh Mikey, we've only just got here. Let's walk round a

46

bit.'

'You can. But I'm buggered; I'll sit here.'

Mikey lit a cigarette and watched his bride as she teetered self-consciously round the square. A pigeon settled on his head. He screamed in a high-pitched voice, then looked at me, ashamed of the undignified sound he had made.

'Well, are you happy now?' he asked his young wife harshly when she returned to his side.

'Why are you mad with me, Mikey?' she asked. 'We're on our honeymoon, you should be happy. *I am*,' she added, unconvincingly.

'I *told* you I hated London, din't I?' he whined.

'But you're not paying for it, are you?' she said. 'Mum and Dad are.'

'Well I tell you what, Emma,' he said, his face getting redder. 'I'd sooner have had the money than London. What will we have to show for it when we get back to Leeds, eh?'

'Happy memories,' she said.

'I'm cold,' he moaned. 'Have you got the key to the room?'

She opened her blue plastic clutch-bag and took out a large, triangular piece of Perspex. A small key hung from one corner.

'It's all key holder and no bloody key,' grumbled Mikey. 'I'm going back; you can do what you like.'

'I'll come with you,' she said, and slid her arm through his. As they walked away she kept looking up at his face. But the tyrant did not smile on his humble subject. He was starting as he meant to go on.

I wanted to run after him and thump him in between his martyred shoulders. I am not normally an aggressive woman. Apart from the one murder I've committed, I've never harmed another person. I blamed my change of mood on hunger and nicotine withdrawal.

I was forced out of the square when a group of American girls wearing wet suits started jumping into the fountains for a dare and splashed passers-by. Some aggrieved wet person called the police, but I left before they could get their big boots out of the van. I headed back up the Charing Cross Road towards my territory. The whole of London was composed of food: 'Big Mac' buildings, pizza pavements, chicken buses, chow mein cars. If people were not eating, they were smoking or drinking or just looking warm. I wanted to cry, but couldn't squeeze a tear out. I started to run, but my heavy duty bra snapped and released my breasts; my cold nipples stuck out like liquorice torpedoes. So I was now forced to walk around with my arms folded. I scanned the pavements looking for a large safety pin, but only found a broken badge which said 'I love London'.

As I walked I could hear a strange, infantile whimpering sound. I looked to right and left, trying to locate the source; I glanced forward and back, but there was nothing there.

8 Family Secrets

After Inspector Sly had gone, John Dakin shut himself in his box-room bedroom and slid the bolt on the door. He could hear Mary, his sister, crying in her own, much bigger bedroom across the landing. He had left his father downstairs sobbing into the Dralon cushions on the sofa. He'd tried to comfort his father by thumping him hard on his heaving shoulders, but his father had not responded, so John had left him to it.

His mother's locked diary was pathetically easy to open. One turn of a screwdriver did it.

Wednesday December 30th

If anyone has found this diary, and is reading it now, I *beg* you to stop. Please put it back where you found it. Still reading? Is it you, Derek, or Mary or John? Whoever it is, please stop.

John read on, nothing would make him stop.

I have decided to live another life. I shall call myself by a different name and on weekdays, between the hours of 9 a.m. and 4 p.m., I shall be another person. In the evening and at weekends I shall be Derek's wife and the children's mother. My new life needn't cost anything. I shall need some sort of disguise. I've lived all my life in this town and too many people know me.

I may call myself Lauren McSkye.

Thursday December 31st

Hello, this is Lauren McSkye. I'm an artist. I haven't painted a picture since leaving school, but I am still an artist.

Friday January 1st

The people I live with are *so* dreary. There is no need for us to have conversations; we all know in advance what each of us is going to say.

Saturday January 2nd

My disguise, bought from Help the Aged charity shop.
Total cost: £3.17p.
Cleopatra wig (black)
Shiny PVC mac (black)
Fedora man's hat (black)
Sunglasses
Mary Quant make-up set (only blue eye-shadow previously used)
    Lauren McSkye has gone away for the weekend. I believe she is sketching, somewhere in Cumbria.

Sunday January 3rd

Lauren is expected back tomorrow morning; after the dreary people have left the house.

Monday January 4th

Hello, I'm back. The drearies are at work, school and college. I helped Coventry with the housework, then packed my clothes into a shopping bag and went into town on the bus. Coventry went into a ladies' lavatory and Lauren came out and made her face up in the mirror over the wash-basin. A person known to Coventry passed Lauren on the way out. To test the disguise Lauren pushed the person aside. The person objected and shouted, 'What's your hurry?' Lauren apologized. Her voice is deeper than Coventry's and has a slight mid-Atlantic accent. Lauren said, 'So sorry, I was miles away. I'm working on a picture. I'm an artist, we tend towards abstraction.'
    The person failed to fully comprehend the explanation,

but was appeased and walked on. The person known to Coventry was her mother-in-law. How Lauren laughed to see such fun and the dish ran away with the spoon.

Tuesday January 5th

Lauren registered for art classes at the Workers' Educational Institute this morning. When asked her name she repeated it many times. 'My name is Lauren McSkye,' she said. 'Lauren as in Bacall, and Skye as in "Over the sea to . . .".'

When asked if she was Ms, Mrs or Miss, Lauren replied, 'I'm none of those things, Lauren McSkye will do.'

She will attend the classes on Mondays and Wednesdays between the hours of 10 a.m. and 12.30 p.m. She will then have lunch in the canteen with her fellow artists.

Wednesday January 6th

Lauren could not attend her first lesson today because one of the drearies has a temperature of a hundred and one and is in bed. Lauren was very angry.

Coventry made the sickly drearie a jugful of lemon and barley. She was, at all times, loving and patient and maternal.

Thursday January 7th

Lauren is impatient to leave the house. She is still angry and resentful but the drearie has the 'flu and Coventry is needed to run up and down the stairs; and Lauren cannot go out without Coventry, can she?

Friday January 8th

Lauren is *demanding* to be allowed out. Coventry is less loving with the drearie.

Saturday January 9th

Lauren is quarrelling non-stop with Coventry. They are both worn out. The drearie is still upstairs and is now complaining of neglect.

Sunday January 10th

Lauren has been screaming 'Let me out. Coventry has spent the day in silence.

Monday January 11th

Lauren went to her first class today. Her fellow students are a mixture of pensioners, redundant executives and unemployed young people.

Lauren's exotic appearance pleased the class. She was considered to be properly artistic-looking. Her refusal to remove her sunglasses was taken for temperament. She is already infatuated with her tutor. His name is Bradford Keynes; he is thin and pale. He has a very long beard and he doesn't care about his clothes. Bradford is passionate about '*line*'. He made the class draw circular shapes. Lauren's shapes managed to look angular. Bradford told her to 'loosen up'.

John stopped reading his mother's diary and reached for his own. He looked up the entries for early January.

John closed both diaries. He felt betrayed and bereaved. He scrubbed at his eyes, but couldn't stop the fat, warm teardrops from dripping down his face. He'd always thought his mother was a nice woman.

9 Dying for a Fag

The traffic lights had broken down at the corner by Centre Point, and a policewoman was trying to control the tangled traffic with elaborate arm wavings and hand waggings and dips of her solid body. I was impressed by these gesticulations and stopped to watch her.

Then I saw that *she* was watching me. Not just watching me, but *noting* me in the special way that the police force have. When she spoke into her little radio I panicked and ran across the road and turned into the first side-street. I didn't look back but as I ran, I imagined that I was being pursued by patrol cars and uniformed officers of the law. I thought it was only a matter of minutes before helicopters with searchlights began swooping over my head.

When I could no longer run I walked, and when walking became impossible I sat down on the steps of the Chest, Heart and Stroke Association to recover. I was in a place called Tavistock Square. Another square. How many more were there?

I counted five cigarette ends on the pavement at the foot of the steps. Perhaps smoking wasn't allowed in the Chest, Heart and Stroke offices. One cigarette had only just been lit before being discarded. Fastidious though I am, I picked it up and held it familiarly between my fingers.

I waited for a woman smoker to appear and asked her for a light. She was old and fat and well dressed, in a scarlet coat and a Paisley shawl.

'Excuse me, can you give me a light?'

'Oh, you *did* frighten me, darting out like that.'

She took a tortoiseshell lighter from her shoulder-bag and clicked it into flame. My face and my right hand were illuminated as I sucked the cigarette alight. She said, 'We're a dying breed, we smokers. One's surprised to meet another nowadays.'

'Yes,' I said. 'This is my first cigarette for twenty-four hours.'

'Tried to give it up, did you?'

I mumbled, 'Couldn't afford it.'

'You *look* as though you're financially embarrassed.'

'I am,' I said.

'I'm going to give you something,' she said, and rummaged inside her bag. She brought out, instead of money, as I'd hoped, a small card engraved:

Celia Heartslove
Financial Clairvoyant to the Stars

'Come and see me when you get back on your feet,' she said. 'I manage Investment Portfolios for household names, and *you* have a positive aura. You're going to *be* somebody. By the way, what *is* that on your face and hands?'

'It's soot,' I said. 'I'm a chimney-sweep.'

She laughed. 'Are there any chimneys left? Well, I *am* surprised. I had my Fallopian tubes tied and my chimneys blocked up years ago. Good night.'

The cigarette warmed me, calmed me down, cheered me up and diminished my hunger pains. As soon as I had finished it I immediately wanted another, so I went in search of one. At a bus stop I found five half-smoked dog-ends on the pavement. I also picked up an empty cigarette packet, half a comb and two and a half pence in change. I felt better now that I had possessions. I put my small acquisitions inside the cigarette box, and was almost cheerful as I walked along the unknown streets. At ten o'clock I stopped in an alley to empty my bowels. I wiped myself clean on dead leaves that had collected against the wall. As I said, I am a fastidious woman.

The rain had left puddles in the cracked pavements, and I dabbled my fingers in them and licked the stony moisture as I journeyed on without a destination.

10 The Local Paper

Bread Knife stared at the front page of the local evening paper. Her daughter's photograph stared back. 'It's in,' she said. And handed the paper to her little round husband.

'Well, I'm disgusted with the whole business,' he said, after silently reading the whole of the front page.

'It's bad blood coming out,' said Bread Knife. This was a reference to her husband's mother, Ruby, a woman now dead but who was known to have frequented violent public houses and had mothered many children. One, a half-caste, now living in Cardiff. Ruby had never married.

So Tennis Ball was illegitimate. He had no idea who his father was and he didn't *want* to know, thank you very much. When Ruby was on her way out, soon to die, she had sent for him, but he hadn't gone, fearing deathbed confessions and sloppy physical contact.

'They say it misses a generation, don't they?' he said.

'Well, it has in this case, hasn't it?' said Bread Knife.

Tennis Ball got up from the sofa and went into the kitchen and placed the newspaper inside the waste-bin under the sink.

Out of sight, out of mind.

KILLER HOUSEWIFE
'COULD STRIKE AGAIN' WARNING
Today residents of the Grey Paths Council Estate were recovering from the shock-revelation that one of their neighbours, Coventry Dakin, was wanted for the murder of Gerald Fox, who was battered to death yesterday. Her husband, Derek Dakin, interviewed by our reporter, Sandra Topping, said, 'My wife has always been a gentle, timid person. I can only think that she is mentally ill.' Asked if he knew of an alleged love tangle between his wife and the murdered man, Mr Dakin commented, 'I don't know what to believe. Coventry has never shown any interest in other men before.'

Balding, bespectacled, neatly dressed Mr Dakin, a supervisor at Hopcroft Shoes Ltd, broke down and wept. 'She would literally not kill a fly; I had to shoo them out of the window with a rolled up newspaper.'

The children of the blonde killer, John, 17, and Mary, 16, are staying with their grandmother, Mrs Edna Dakin, in her pensioner's bungalow. 'She was a dark horse,' said Mrs Dakin. 'Nobody ever knew what she was thinking.'

Asked if Mrs Dakin was surprised that her daughter-in-law was wanted for murder, Mrs Dakin replied, 'Not really.'

The wife of the murdered man, Mrs Carole Fox, was today under deep sedation in hospital. Her children, who witnessed the horrific slaying, are being cared for by friends. Mr D. J. Broadway, headmaster of John Kennedy Primary School, where the children are pupils, said: 'I expect they will be off school for a few days.' Asked to comment on the murder he said: 'Grey Paths Estate has no community centre; people have nothing to do in the evening.'

The County Police Force have issued the following description of Coventry Dakin: 'She is 5′8″ tall, of slim build, with blonde hair and brown eyes. When last seen she was wearing blue bell-bottom trousers and a grey sweatshirt printed with a tortoise design.'

A police spokesman added: 'One theory for the murder motive is that Coventry Dakin struck out in anger after Gerald Fox told her that their affair was over. Another is that Coventry Dakin is a member of a fanatical feminist undercover group who are pledged to eradicate men.' When asked what evidence he had to sustain such a startling theory, the spokesman said, 'Several informants have come forward and Dakin was known to have blackened her face in terrorist fashion before battering Gerald Fox to death.' He warned, 'She could strike again.'

11 Coventry Tittie

Around midnight on Thursday, I had a rush of optimism to the head. Perhaps he's alive. How could a silly plastic doll kill a six-foot overweight man? I pulled a newspaper I'd never heard of out of a litter-bin, the *Standard*. There was no mention of me murdering a man; perhaps the London press was not interested in provincial murder, though they had reported other violent deaths: people crushed by farm machinery, trapped inside burning lorries, drowned in quarries.

After I'd finished reading the paper I shoved it inside my sweat-shirt where it served two purposes: it kept me warm, and acted as a nipple guard. I haven't mentioned it before but, dirty and badly dressed as I was, I had been propositioned by many men as I trudged along the pavements. All of the men looked respectable and ordinary. Some had opened car doors and invited me into the passenger seat. Some of the cars had baby seats in the back. I wondered why such men should try to pick up a smelly stranger, when most of them would surely have a fragrant wife at home. But then I remembered that my figure was outlined clearly by the clothes I was wearing. I was a collection of female hormones on the move, and served to remind men of their basic biological needs and desires. Nobody ever takes a beautiful woman seriously, apart from herself.

My good looks have always been a source of shame to my parents. When I was a child they deliberately brutalized my appearance. My blonde curls were hacked off or hidden under unflattering knitted caps. My body was clothed in an over-large school uniform during the week, complete with clumpy lace-up shoes. At the weekends I wore shrunken cardigans and floppy pleated skirts.

I was a freak at an early age. My breasts started to grow at an alarming rate when I was twelve. One moment I was running around playing games in the school playground and, it seemed, the next I was huddled in a corner with my back stooped and my arms folded over my chest. During the hottest summer I wore a cardigan; games became an ordeal; showers were torture. I ran through the steaming room with my eyes closed. It was a tall, thin, jealous girl called Tania Draycock who first changed my nickname from 'Coventry City' to 'Coventry Tittie'. By the age of fifteen my breasts were enormous; even harnessed and bound they protruded through my clothes. They affronted people. Teachers flicked their eyes away in alarm, strangers stared in fascination.

My relations were plain people who didn't believe in hair ribbons or coloured shoes. Their clothes were chosen for camouflage rather than adornment. So at sixteen, when I became a beatnik, the attraction was not intellectual but practical. Beatniks wore huge bosom-concealing sloppy sweaters and duffel-coats. For the first time in years I was able to relax. I stopped stooping and unfolded my arms and started to read the books that I had been carrying around under my arm as part of my uniform.

Sometimes my looks were helpful. They got me a job as an office junior in a cardboard box factory. I had no other qualifications. 'Take your coat off, dear,' Mr Ridgely said. 'It's 'ot in 'ere.' I was young and trusting. I took my coat off . . . folded my arms. Mr Ridgely's brow became covered in sweat which he patted dry with a maroon handkerchief. 'I tell you what, would you mind standing on my desk and opening that top window?'

I had no experience of men. I stood on the desk and was surprised to find that Mr Ridgely had not moved from his chair. I leaned forward to open the window, an icy wind rushed into the room and blew papers about. Mr Ridgely was looking up my skirt. Our eyes met, the maroon handkerchief came out again.

'Yes, you'll do,' he said. 'Start on Monday.'

For the next two years I continued to believe that Mr Ridgely had looked up my skirt accidentally. I also thought that he was an unusually clumsy man, constantly brushing against me and falling in my path. Once, when putting up the office Christmas decorations, he had fallen off a ladder on top of me. We lay sprawled on the lino, he still on top of me. Mr Ridgely took too long in getting to his feet.

'Let's just lie like this, together, for a while, shall we?' he muttered into my neck. 'I'm tired. I need a rest. My wife is very demanding; she won't let me sleep.'

Being very young and stupid I'd thought he meant that his wife insisted on him doing DIY until the early hours. I imagined Mr Ridgely insulating his loft by torchlight.

12 On the Beach

'Christ, I'm starving!' said Sidney. 'How much longer?'

Sidney and Ruth were sitting in an open-sided shack which was on a beach near to Albufeira. They had given their order to a distracted middle-aged woman in a print dress an hour and a half previously. They had not seen her since. A small child had served them bread, butter and sliced tomatoes. Then the child had disappeared, shrieking, into the sea.

The cook, a manic extrovert, wore a sea captain's hat, a skimpy bathing pouch and orange flip-flops. During this time he had done no cooking. Instead, he'd been drawing water from a well in a bucket and throwing the contents over the heads and tables of his Portuguese customers. His fancy was then to force his sodden customers to rise to their feet and box with him. After that he embraced them and shouted for a bottle before sitting down at their wet table to have a drink.

Ruth said: 'It must be a local custom, Sid.'

Sidney said: 'If he chucks a bucket of water over me I'll drop him one. That's *our* custom in the East Midlands.'

Ruth sighed and looked at the view, which was almost as good as the brochure had promised. There it was: pale yellow sand, dramatic orange rocks, light blue sky and dark blue sea. The brochure had recommended that they try one of the beach shack restaurants; the piri-piri chicken was supposed to be 'mouth-wateringly good'.

A few insects fell from the woven grass roof onto Sidney's head. Ruth watched them scampering around in his hair, but she didn't say anything. She was too hot and couldn't be bothered. On the other side of the shack the cook rose to his feet, threw his head back and balanced a glass of brandy on his forehead. A toothless old woman dressed in black started to clap and soon everyone in the shack, apart from Sidney and Ruth, was on their feet, swaying and stamping on the crude boarded floor, encouraging the cook.

'I've never seen such a show-off,' whispered Ruth.

Sidney mouthed: 'He's coming over, look away!'

Too late. The cook was approaching their rickety table for two. Then his brown, hairy belly was brushing against Ruth's fair, English arm.

'OK, Americans?' bellowed the cook.

'No,' shouted Sidney. 'We're not OK, and we're English and we want our food.'

'Ah Ingleeshe, Bobby Charlton – yes?'

'Yes!' said Sidney, who hated football.

'President Reagan – yes?'

'No,' said Sidney, 'Margaret Thatcher.'

'Winston Churchill?'

'He's dead,' said Sidney. '*Morto*.'

'Princess Di . . . Rolls Royce?'

'Yes, and while you're here, old cock, piri-piri chicken please, for two, with potatoes and a salad and a cold bottle of *vinho verde*. That is, if it's not too much trouble. I mean we've only been waiting nearly two bloody hours, watching you prat around, you big tub of lard.' Sidney said all this with a charming smile. The cook took the glass from his forehead, drank the contents and gave Sidney a friendly thump on the head, which hurt Sidney and killed the insects. The cook shouted harsh instructions to the toothless crone who caught a passing chicken, and strangled it, after a short struggle.

Within another half hour pieces of the unfortunate chicken were spitting on the barbecue and cutlery had been brought to the table. A bottle of delicately green wine dripping with condensation was put before them. The small child emerged from the sea, went into the kitchen and brought them a large, crisp salad. The crone laid down a dish of small, steaming potatoes still in their skins. Salt and pepper appeared, then curls of melting butter, and finally the chicken, succulent and crisp-edged and smelling of lemons and garlic.

They started to eat and were at least halfway through their meal before a bucket of ice-cold water washed the food off their plates.

13 Calcutta

To be hungry is to feel an emptiness in the belly, but the worst thing about hunger is the feeling of panic inside the head. I am getting desperate, the idea of stealing food is no longer unthinkable. I am growing cunning . . . I am a fox; my eyes are narrowing and are fixed on a bunch of bananas which are just inside the door of a twenty-four-hour supermarket. The grocer, a beautiful Asian boy, is reading an Indian-language newspaper. He looks a kind boy; I don't want to steal from him. I go into the shop and ask him for a banana.

The fluorescent lights expose my sooty face and hands. The boy looks up; he is alarmed.

'Bananas are twenty-five pence each,' he says and adds, 'regardless of size.'

I select a banana, the largest of the bunch. I take it to the checkout. He rings up twenty-five pence on the till and holds his hand out. I give him two and a half pence.

'I've got no more money, I'm very hungry.'

'Sorry,' he says, shaking his glossy head. 'You are the third tonight to ask.'

'I'll pay you back,' I plead.

'No.'

'I beg you.'

'No. Go away.'

I peel the skin from the banana.

Before I can get it to my mouth he snatches it from me. I snatch it back. The banana slips and slithers between us and eventually disintegrates and falls onto discarded till rolls on the floor. He wipes his sticky hands on his short overall with small cries of disgust.

'You are a dirty cow,' he says. 'And a thief.'

'I'm hungry,' I say. 'I've never been so hungry before.'

'Good, so now you know,' he shouts. 'I am from Calcutta. There *everybody* is hungry.'

A white-haired Indian man comes out of the back of the shop. He wears the expression of someone at the end of his tether. The boy gathers the wasted banana together and throws it into a bin underneath the counter.

He could have given it to me after all.

14 Heartbreak House

Derek Dakin sat on the marital bed and removed his trousers, socks and shoes. He had some trouble untying his shoe laces because his hands were trembling. He got up and opened the wardrobe door and hung his folded trousers carefully over a wooden coat-hanger on the right side of the hanging rail.

Coventry's clothes, careful and respectable, hung on the left side. Derek touched each article of Coventry's clothing. He then buried his face in the brown sleeve of her eleven-year-old winter coat. He sniffed hard and smelt a vague smell of Tramp (the perfume he'd bought her for Christmas). Its sweetness was intermingled with the rancid smell of the cigarettes she smoked.

He had always known that one day his wife would leave him, though he had not expected murder to be the motivating factor in her decision.

He thought, she was so beautiful and *good*. Whereas he was very plain-looking (even before he lost most of his hair) and he was *not* good. He was riddled with faults. He harboured grudges and spent too much time with his tortoises.

Derek took Coventry's winter coat off the hanger and put it on. It fitted him perfectly. He looked into the full-length wardrobe mirror and watched himself as he fastened the knobbly little buttons up to the neck. Derek then squeezed his bare feet into Coventry's brown, high-heeled court shoes. He wobbled over to the chest of drawers and found a headscarf and a pair of gloves. He put them on. While he was there he squirted himself with Tramp. He looked through Coventry's dressing-table drawers and found a stub of pink lipstick and slashed the cloying stuff across his lips. He went back to the mirror and looked at himself through half-closed eyes. But it was no good. However hard he tried he couldn't make Coventry appear in front of him.

He undressed and put her things away. As he did so he thought, 'My heart *is* breaking.' He could feel that organ, so long associated with love and romance, tearing away from whatever kept it in place.

'I shall die of a broken heart,' he said in a whisper to himself.

He put his pyjamas on over his underpants and got into bed on Coventry's side. He clutched her pillow to him as though it were Coventry herself. He moaned, 'Coventry, Coventry,' into the depths of the curled duck feathers of which the pillow was composed.

It was Derek's habit before he went to sleep to talk Coventry through the happenings of his day. Sometimes Coventry went to sleep before he'd finished. When this happened Derek would lie at her side and look at her perfect face and congratulate himself on having this exquisite woman for his wife.

Sometimes he would carefully draw back the sheets and blankets and Coventry's nightdress and gaze at his wife's naked body. In doing this he was not activated by desire. Sex had played only a walk-on part in their lives together. It had never been centre stage. No, he was content to look and experience the power of possession.

He couldn't live without Coventry. She protected him from the world and its many humiliations. He would probably die in his sleep tonight. His heart was breaking into pieces, had come loose from its moorings. He could feel it distinctly now, as it tugged and struggled to be free.

He imagined John, his son, phoning around to the relations. 'Bad news. Dad's dead. He died in the night of a broken heart.' Tears ran into the pillow as Derek imagined the grieving relations, his orphaned children; his body inside the coffin; his workmates wearing suits and black ties, standing at the open grave, sorry now for the torment they had put him through on the shop floor so often.

He fantasized about the two-minute silence there would be at the next meeting of the Tortoise Society. Bob Bridges, the chairman, would break the stillness by saying: 'Derek Dakin knew his tortoises.' High praise from Bob, who knew *his* tortoises.

But best of all, when she heard of his death, Coventry would come back and throw herself on his freshly earthed grave. She would blame herself and rip her hair out and rend her clothing and refuse to move, until forced to by the authorities.

Derek was almost disappointed when he opened his eyes and found himself still alive, with the bedroom lights blazing and his face and teeth unwashed. He got out of bed and crossed the landing. A light shone under the bathroom door. He tried the door; it was locked.

'Won't be long,' shouted John. Derek walked impatiently up and down the small landing. He straightened a few pictures of steam trains, then the bathroom door opened and John came out.

'God, Dad, you look awful.'

Derek said: 'I'm entitled to look awful, aren't I? Your mother's committed a murder and run off.'

'I didn't mean that, Dad. It was just a bit of a shock to see you wearing lipstick.'

Derek said: 'It's your mother's lipstick. I was . . .'

'Look, there's no problem. Don't feel you have to explain. It's cool. This is nineteen eighty-eight. The lipstick is great and so is the perfume.'

John watched a great deal of American soap opera drama and knew what to say and do. So he hugged his father and said again: 'It's cool,' and shut himself in his bedroom.

Derek went into the bathroom and removed the lipstick with a face flannel. When his lips were rubbed clean he came out of the bathroom and knocked on John's door.

'John, it's Dad. I want to explain.'

Mary came out of her bedroom. Her pretty face was swollen and red from a marathon crying session. 'What's up?' she asked. 'Have you heard from Mum?'

'No,' said Derek. 'Go back to sleep.'

John opened his door. He avoided looking at Derek's face.

'I can't go to sleep,' said Mary. 'I want my mum.'

The three of them stood on the landing in their nightclothes. Nobody knew what to say or do. Mary felt bereaved twice over. For three years she'd had a violent crush on Gerald Fox. He had never known about her love for him and now he never would.

Eventually, after an awkward silence, Coventry's family went to their respective beds.

15 Over in Three Minutes

WANTED. HELP IN RATHER UNCONVENTIONAL HOUSEHOLD.
LIVE-IN. SMOKER PREFERRED.
APPLY IN PERSON TO PROFESSOR WILLOUGHBY D'ERESBY,
BUT PLEASE DON'T INTERRUPT EASTENDERS.
GOWER STREET. NO NUMBER, ALAS, BUT LOOK FOR
LARGE URN OUTSIDE FRONT DOOR.

I was staring at Professor Willoughby D'Eresby's advertisement in a newsagent's window when a man with an executive brief-case came and stood by my side. It was five o'clock in the morning. The street was shiny black and deserted. The newsagent's window spilt yellow light onto the man's black lace-up shoes. He cleared his throat.

'Are you a business girl?'

'Yes, I'm a self-employed chimney-sweep.'

He looked at me. He had a nice, stupid face. He was disappointed. 'Sorry to bother you.'

He turned away and walked down the street. His shoes clicked loudly on the pavement.

He walked like a man who had nowhere to go. I clung to the pool of light and watched him. He turned around and looked at me. We stared at each other for a few seconds. London had defeated me. I was mad from hunger and terror. He walked back to me, swinging his brief-case. He said very quietly: 'Have you got anywhere to go?'

'No, have you?'

'No.'

'A park?'

'Yes, all right.'

'It's not too cold?'

'No.'

He held my hand; he'd been drinking. He asked me my name. I refused to tell him. He said his name was Leslie and that he'd missed his train. Three of his teeth were missing. We walked without speaking until we came to a square. The gates were locked.

'Can you jump over the railings?' he asked, in his quiet voice. I answered him by pulling on the overhanging branch of a tree and, using it to steady myself, onto the top of the railings. I balanced on them for some time, comfortable in my old clothes and shoes; ready to leap and run and turn somersaults in the grass.

It took him longer to climb over. He was careful and slow and I said, 'You've only got one decent suit, haven't you?'

'The one I'm wearing,' he said. 'My interview suit. I didn't get the job, though,' he added. When we were in the park he held my hand again. 'I don't like the dark,' he said. The trees swayed overhead as we lay down together. It started to rain.

'I can smell soot,' he said.

'It's me,' I said.

He took his white shirt off and put it, carefully folded, inside his brief-case. He started to tremble in the cold. I told him to put his suit jacket back on.

'No,' he said. 'We'll soon be warm.'

We lay together in the rain for a few quiet moments, and then he asked politely if I was ready to start. We started, went on and finished. It was all over in three minutes. His wet string vest shone in the dark under his breathless back. 'Well, that was very nice,' he said as we separated and became two bodies again.

'Thank you,' I said.

We could have been talking about a slice of home-made cake. As the sky lightened we discussed my fee. 'I've only got a few quid,' he said, and turned his pockets inside out, as though I had called him a liar. For further proof he opened his brief-case. I looked inside.

'Can I have the cigarettes and the Kit-Kat please?' I asked.

'Yes,' he said, 'and I can spare two pounds.'

He handed the coins to me and I pressed them to my cheek. I ate the Kit-Kat and smoked a cigarette while Leslie told me about his wife and how much he loved her. The day had crept up unnoticed. It was light. We stood up.

'I didn't know you were so lovely,' he said. 'Is your hair natural?'

'No, it's a wig,' I said and ran towards the railings, scaled them and was off, running, to find Professor Willoughby D'Eresby's house.

16 Unconventional Household

'Pronounce it Darby,' coughed Professor Willoughby D'Eresby, as he stood on the top doorstep of his house in Gower Street looking at me. 'I say, you're splendidly dirty, aren't you? Like traffic, do you, noise and smell of?'

'No.'

'Pity, I'm very partial to the smell of diesel and, my dear, I'm in *seventh heaven* if a juggernaut crashes its gears outside my study window. Odd, isn't it?'

He looked happily up and down Gower Street at the snarling rush-hour traffic, inhaled deeply on the fumes, then flung his lighted cigarette stub into an urn by the door containing hundreds of fellow stubs and nodded me into the interior of the house. He immediately lit another cigarette, coughed, choked and, with watering eyes, said, 'Is that a Benson you're smoking?'

'Yes,' I said.

'Thought so. Got a frightfully good nose for a fag.'

The professor's super-refined upper-class accent sounded like a foreign language. When he spoke I had to strain to understand him.

As I was about to enter the kitchen, he put a restraining hand on my arm. 'Perhaps I ought to tell you that my wife is a psychologist and she doesn't wear clothes in the house.'

From the kitchen came the sound of wild laughter and then a shrill voice shouting, 'Stop pissing about, Gerard, and bring her in. She's seen a naked *woman* before.'

'You're swearing again, Letitia, and it's not yet noon.'

Professor Willoughby D'Eresby pulled me into the kitchen and towards his wife, who put the *Guardian* down and revealed her head and torso and breasts. It took me a few seconds to recover, but I managed to say, 'Hello.'

'Sit yourself down, my dear,' she said. 'I expect you want a few quiet moments in which to recover. Shocking sight, aren't I?'

I thought it best to say nothing.

'I admire my wife enormously,' said the professor defensively.

'She does as she pleases, you know.'

'Within the law, Gerard,' added Letitia, lighting a large cigar.

'Oh yes, within the law,' drawled her husband.

I glanced around the kitchen. Flies had colonized the sink. The cardboard remains of Marks & Spencer's oriental dinners for two were thrown about the floor. Ashtrays contained insecure pyramids of cigar butts and cigarette ends. Milk bottles contained penicillin-like substances.

I sat at the kitchen table with my feet sticking to the floor. I tried not to breathe. Somewhere a drain was blocked. Letitia Willoughby D'Eresby started to read aloud an item from the *Guardian*, something about child abuse. Her husband listened attentively, saying: 'Awful! awful!' every now and again. An evil-looking cat loped in, worrying a half-dead mouse. It deposited it at Letitia's feet.

'Ah look, darling! Thatcher has brought you in a little present!'

'Thank you, Thatcher, you old bastard,' said Letitia. Then, 'OK . . . we can't keep this gorgeous child waiting a moment longer.'

She threw the *Guardian* onto the floor and turned to me. I glimpsed grey pubic hair and mottled thighs as she raised herself to turn her chair to face me. I shut my eyes. . . . 'As you can see, we're lazy sods. We do no housework. We can't cook. We smoke compulsively and I walk around displaying my clapped-out old tits. Can't keep domestic help, can we, Gerard? . . .'

'Can't *get* domestic help, darling,' said Gerard, smiling fondly at his moustachioed wife.

Letitia smiled back and continued: 'We'll give you forty pounds a week and free board, if you'll keep us straight and cook us a meal every now and again . . . How say you?'

'I say yes.'

'Oh, that's supercalafragilistic!' said Letitia.

'Wife!' boomed Gerard. 'You're never to use that word again in my hearing. It's twee, it's regressive and *it is not a proper word*.'

'Did you see *Mary Poppins*?' Letitia asked me eagerly.

'Four times,' I said.

'I've seen it eleven times at the pictures, and fuck knows how many times on video. I find its naïve – not to say moronic – simplicity to be utterly enchanting.' Her voice changed, her eyes narrowed. She turned on her husband. 'And it sodding well really *is* a proper word, it's in the *Oxford English Dictionary* . . . I think! And if it's not, it jolly well ought to be. As well you know, I use it on a daily basis.'

She stood up. I closed my eyes.

'Right, Gerard, get up them bleeding stairs!' she said.

Letitia and Gerard wheezed up the stairs in front of me. I watched Letitia's buttocks with great interest as they swayed and dimpled and generally behaved like two grey blancmanges on the move. As we turned the stairs towards the attic floor, I thought, 'I wish Derek could see me now, with my nose only inches away from Letitia's bare bum.'

The thought of Derek being here in this house at all made me laugh out loud, and my companions turned and laughed with me; but asked for no explanation.

'We never come up here,' said Letitia, unnecessarily, as she looked around at the two tidy rooms and ash-free carpets. 'So you can do your own thing, play your pop records, practise body-popping . . . or whatever it is you young people do.'

'I'm nearly forty,' I said: the first piece of information I had volunteered.

They had not asked me for my name or my circumstances.

'If you'd wear your glasses, Letitia, you would have seen the tiny wrinkles on this dear girl's face. Vanity, Letitia, vanity.'

Professor Willoughby D'Eresby stroked his wife's buttocks fondly. They stood in reverie for a few moments and then Letitia wobbled about, opening windows and skylights and apologizing for the graffiti on the white walls.

GET OUT WHILE YOU CAN!
CAROLINE

SHE'S A LOONY. HE'S A NUTTER.
JOANNE

WATCH OUT FOR THE SON.
GLORIA

Gerard smiled at the writing on the walls. 'We're used to being called "nutters", aren't we, darling?'

'Oh yes,' smiled Letitia. 'I used to work with Ronnie Laing.'

'So you've a son?' I enquired.

Their faces clouded over. They looked old and dirty and smelly.

70

Their shoulders drooped, they sighed.

'Keir,' said Professor Willoughby D'Eresby, sadly.

'He's very hard to reach. He's in a state of ontological insecurity,' added his wife.

'Where does he live?' I asked, suddenly nervous.

'Floor below,' said Willoughby D'Eresby, lighting another cigarette and flinging the discarded stub of his previous cigarette into the sparkling wash-basin. 'We must go to work. Here, get yourself whatever you need, abrasive powders, black plastic bags . . .' His voice trailed off; he was on uncertain domestic ground. He searched his suit for money and pulled out a bundle of fifty-pound notes.

'Ooh, can I have one of those, darling?' asked Letitia.

He gave us one each and they went downstairs to prepare for work. Mad Keir was much on my mind.

I bolted the attic door and sat on my bed. I had nothing to put in the chest of drawers or the matching pine wardrobe. I had no face flannel to display or soap to arrange. I was simply . . . there, in that most traditional of fugitives' hiding places, the attic.

I heard the front door slam and poked my head out of the skylight window, hoping to see the Willoughby D'Eresbys. Professor Willoughby D'Eresby came into view, crossing Gower Street with a smart, middle-aged woman on his arm. She was wearing a fashionable padded-shouldered suit in a grey checked material. She teetered on black high-heeled court shoes and she carried a bulging black brief-case. She said something and, as they both laughed, she turned her head. It was Letitia Willoughby D'Eresby, in clothes and scarlet lipstick.

They walked out of sight and I was very sorry to see them go.

I was now alone in the house with Keir.

I pressed my ear to the carpet and listened hard. I could hear no wild mutterings or crazed monologue from the floor below. Perhaps he raved through the night, and slept during the day. I hoped so.

I was too frightened of Keir to be able to luxuriate in a bath. Instead I took my clothes off and washed at the wash-basin in my room. One of the previous occupants had left behind a little bottle of Marks & Spencer's liquid soap. I pressed the plunger joyfully over and over until the bottle signalled it was empty by making a digusting noise. I washed away the soot, the tears, the rain, the sweat and Leslie's semen from the night before. I washed until I was gloriously renewed and all my tribulations and all my sins had trickled down the waste-pipe and disappeared underground. Then, having no others, I put on my dirty clothes and started to work.

They hadn't left me a key but it didn't matter because the lock to the front door was broken; so I came and went all day, shopping and taking out the rubbish and lining clean milk bottles up on the step. I ate non-stop: fruit, sweets, crisps, two pork pies. But I didn't buy a newspaper. To read about myself and my crime in black and white would make it real. I rang Sidney every hour, but got no reply.

I found a cooker, a fridge and a dishwasher in the kitchen, all out of action due to encrustations of dirt or ice. It was deeply satisfying getting them all to work and I quite forgot Keir for ten minutes at a time. The remainder of the time I spent looking over my shoulder and waiting for an axe to fall between my shoulder blades. I was scraping grease off the kitchen wall with a fish slice when the Willoughby D'Eresbys returned. They made no comment on the spectacular renewal of their domestic appliances. They were deep in conversation. They flung their coats onto the newly scrubbed kitchen table and ignored me.

'But, Letitia, the Tsarevich's haemophilia was the cause of Alexandra's depression and subsequent religious fervour. You're being very silly to try to prove that it was a simple case of post-natal depression.'

Letitia unbuttoned her blouse. 'Rasputin took advantage of that poor woman during a time of hormonal upheaval. Hello, my dear, have you been busy? It's very light in here.' She looked around, bemused. She took off her skirt.

'I cleaned the windows,' I said, getting to my feet. The rest of the wall would have to wait. I threw the fish slice into the sink.

'I've never seen that before,' said Professor Willoughby D'Eresby, pointing in astonishment at the newly scrubbed kitchen floor with its mock terracotta tiles. Letitia examined it as she unhooked her bra.

'Of course you have; it's been down at least seven years. We chose it together . . . from Habitat. When we were paying for it a man had an epileptic fit on a pile of dhurries,' she prompted.

'Remember now,' said Willoughby D'Eresby. 'You pushed a lollipop stick into his mouth and splintered his tongue.'

I took a casserole dish out of the oven and put it on the newly scrubbed table. I had expected amazed cries and perhaps a jump or two of joy, but the Willoughby D'Eresbys sat down at the table and slopped the beef casserole onto their plates without comment. They were not discreet eaters; they smacked their lips, gravy dribbled down their chins unchecked and unnoticed. Letitia finished first.

'Any afters?'

'A rice pudding,' I said and got up and took it out of the oven. It was perfect: brown crispy skin concealed a creamy bed of plump rice. Professor Willoughby D'Eresby said quickly: 'Bags I the skin.'

Letitia shouted: 'No, bags *I* the skin.'

The rice pudding dish, though hot, was pulled to and fro across the table.

Keir came into the kitchen. '*Où sont les cigarettes?*' he said.

'Speak English in front of the housekeeper, dear,' said Letitia. 'She is uneducated.'

Keir glanced at me without interest. He was a very tall, bare-foot man in his early twenties. His matted dark hair fell onto his shoulders and framed a face like a thin grey pillow. A pair of dark blue workman's overalls hung from his emaciated body. His toenails needed cutting. He didn't look capable of lifting an axe, let alone going berserk with one. Letitia handed him her cigarettes and he took them and went out of the kitchen without speaking another word.

'He's stopped eating properly,' said the professor, breaking the silence.

'Since when?' I asked.

'Since he was seventeen and we packed him off to Oxford,' said Letitia.

'He was quite astonishingly clever, y'see,' cut in her husband, 'but he didn't want to go. We had to *prise* him out of the car and into Balliol. He made an awful scene on the stairs outside his room, said some quite *unforgettable* things to his mother, accused her of abandoning him.'

'We'd never spent a night apart,' explained Letitia.

'Within a fortnight the poor boy had regressed to a state of chaotic nonentity and he has never properly recovered.'

'But he *must* eat *something*,' I insisted. 'I mean, if he didn't he'd die, wouldn't he?'

Willoughby D'Eresby drew heavily on his cigarette and, marking his points by tapping on the table with his dessert spoon, said: 'But he doesn't eat with us. He never leaves this house. No food is ever missing. And nobody ever calls to see him. So you see, my dear, it's a mystery to us why he is still alive but he is.'

'Has he seen a doctor?' I asked.

'Oh no, he'd hate that,' said Letitia. 'He has entirely negative feelings towards the medical profession.'

'He looks very poorly,' I ventured. 'Very thin and undernourished.'

'Well he's bound to, isn't he?' said Professor Willoughby D'Eresby with an air of finality, 'if he doesn't eat.'

'*Eastenders*,' said Letitia. And they got up from the table and, knocking chairs over in their haste, they rushed from the kitchen and into the sitting-room. I stacked the dishwasher, and from the hallway then dialled the familiar telephone number connecting me to Sidney's villa: 010 351 89 . . . He was in.

'Sidney? It's me!' I was shouting with relief.

'Coventry? I've just had the police onto me. They reckon you've killed one of your neighbours.'

'Yes, I have, Sidney. What did the police say?'

'They wanted to know if you'd phoned me. I told them I'd had the phone off all day. We've only just got out of bed,' he added. 'Coventry, you've made a balls-up of the twelfth commandment, haven't you?'

'What's that?' I said.

'Thou shalt love thy neighbour as thyself,' he laughed down the phone.

'Sidney, I'm in London, but don't tell anyone; do you promise?'

'Even Derek?'

'Especially Derek.'

'Don't come out to Portugal, will you, Cov? I've got a week left and I want to enjoy it without complications. I'll help you when I get back, but I just want this week, OK?'

'How could I, Sid? I've got no money, no passport or . . .'

'Good. Ring me when I get back . . . at the shop.' He inhaled on his cigarette, then said, 'Did this neighbour you killed deserve to die?' He asked this as casually as someone might say, 'Sugar?'

'No,' I said. 'He deserved to have a nasty bang on the head but he didn't deserve to die. I shouldn't have killed him.' A manic woman cut in and said something in what I presumed to be Portuguese. Then the phone went dead.

A voice behind me said, 'Who have you killed?'

74

It was Keir; he was chewing on a rolled-up copy of *Private Eye*. He swallowed a cartoon while he waited for me to reply. Eventually I said: 'You're very ill, you know.'

'But not mad,' he replied. 'Not like them in there.'

He turned and went slowly back upstairs to his room. I put the phone down and went upstairs and knocked on Keir's door. He opened it at once: 'I knew it would be you.'

'Can I come in?'

'No. Nobody ever comes in.'

Grey feathers floated about on the bare boards under his feet.

'Has your pillow burst?' I asked him, indicating the feathery floor.

'No, stupid, these are pigeon feathers,' he said. 'I'm surprised you didn't identify them immediately. Doesn't everybody keep pigeons in the north?'

'No. So I can't come in?'

'No.'

'And you won't come out?'

'No. No need. Not now I've got my fags.'

He closed his door. A feather escaped from his room and descended the stairs. On my way down I picked it up. There was a smear of blood on the quill shaft.

I put my head round the sitting-room door. My employers were sitting on a sofa shaped like an oyster shell. They were engrossed in a TV conversation going on between black and white cockneys. I shouted, 'I'm going to have a bath.' Willoughby D'Eresby gave a Hitler salute of acknowledgement and I backed out. There was no lock on the bathroom door but I barricaded myself in with an Ali Baba basket and a pile of books.

Earlier in the day I had cleaned the bath and wash-basin and had emptied three bottles of bleach down the foetid lavatory. But there was nothing I could do about the ragged coconut matting prickling under my feet or the topographical shapes of mildew that crept around the walls. The water trickled lethargically out of the hot tap, accompanied by banging in the pipes. I've never been in a more inconvenient household. Hardly anything worked; or if it did, it only worked the *second* time and was accompanied by noise or smoke or slight electric shocks. In that house even pressing a light switch took courage.

I looked around for soap. I found five slivers stuck together at the bottom of a jam jar. After ten minutes there were still only a few inches of water in the bath; but I couldn't wait. I took my filthy clothes off and got in.

My bathroom at home is cosy and has a matching avocado suite, set off well with brown and beige contrasting towels. Recently Derek made a clever shelf that fits above the wash-basin. He used his jigsaw to cut out convenient shapes for the family's toothbrushes . . . Each slot is labelled with the owner's name: MUMMY, DADDY, JOHN, MARY. I mentioned to Derek that my name is not 'Mummy' but he hates 'Coventry' and refuses to use it. He's called me 'Mummy' since John was born seventeen years ago. Derek once said, 'I'm a laughing stock at work because of your name.'

But I know that my name is not the reason for any hilarity that greets him on the shop floor: Derek is. His most famous boring monologue is 'How to boil the perfect egg'. What should, by nature, have taken at most four minutes in the telling, in Derek's mouth became an epic and is now legend and myth. Everyone who was within earshot in the factory remembers the day Derek delivered his boiled egg lecture. Just as they remember where they were when J.R. was shot. That afternoon at clocking-out time one of his workmates was heard to say, 'If that bleedin' Derek opens his trap tomorrow, I'll crack *his* egg-head open *and* I'll pour salt in the cavity an' all!'

To be fair to Derek he has got an unpopular job. He is a chaser in a shoe factory, Hopcroft Shoes Ltd. It is his function to track down orders in the various manufacturing departments and then nag the various foremen and forewomen to hurry the order through. He takes his responsibilities very seriously and will be awake at night worrying that twenty dozen cossack boots are still kicking their heels in the finishing room waiting for their buckles, when they should have been on sale in the Co-op shoe department two days before.

We always used to go to Hopcroft's Annual Dinner and Dance, but we were never invited to join the big, noisy tables where people were obviously enjoying themselves. Instead we sat at a table for four with a senile retired worker and his wife. Last year Derek talked solidly throughout the whole of the turkey dinner. His subject was tortoise gestation. The old couple listened uncomprehendingly, as I did myself.

His nickname at work is 'Boring Derek'. I know this because as the dinner progressed to dance and Derek's workmates became intoxicated with alcohol and atmosphere, they shouted: 'Get out the way: here comes Boring Derek.' A path as wide as a sheep drover's road opened before us. At such times I felt sorry for Derek and wanted to protect him. I half fell in love with him again and kissed his neck when we were dancing. When the balloons were released from their net at the end of the evening, I dived into the mob and grabbed the biggest I could find and presented it to Derek. Like a mother placating an unpopular child.

We always made love after the Annual Dinner and Dance. Derek talked all the way through, asking me questions about the various men who attended the function. His fantasy was that the managing director, Mr Sibson (a man of twenty-three stone), and I were copulating on the dance floor, surrounded by his workmates doing the hokey-cokey.

I married Derek because I was in love with him. I was eighteen.

17 Norman Hartnell with Plimsolls

Letitia Willoughby D'Eresby pushed the bathroom door open and fell over the barrier of books. A mildewed face flannel crunched under her hand as she scrambled to her feet. I was sitting in the bath dyeing my hair dark auburn with a do-it-yourself kit I'd bought in a hardware shop during the day. Gobbets of dye were dropping from my head, onto my body and into the bathwater, staining it blood-red. Letitia opened her mouth and screamed, 'For Christ's sake, Gerard, come in here at once! The hired help's topped herself.' She then leapt at the artery under my throat and pressed hard with her big, broad thumbs.

It was some time before I was able to explain to the Willoughby D'Eresbys that it was a change of appearance I was hoping to achieve, rather than translation into another world. In the confusion I left the dye on too long and my hair is now the colour of a particularly tangy satsuma. The W.D.s approve of this dramatic change in my appearance. Letitia said, 'You must wear green,' and she has given me a pair of jade earrings she bought in Indonesia. They are four inches long. She offered to pierce my ears with a darning needle and a cork but I declined this kindness.

I have thrown my chimney-sweeping clothes away and am now wearing a Norman Hartnell mohair suit which Letitia last wore in 1959, when she was a size ten. It is luxuriously soft, with a navy sheen though, of course, it doesn't look at its best with plimsolls.

That night I lay awake for hours thinking about my children. When I eventually slept, I dreamt of being in prison. I was sharing a cell with Ruth Ellis. We were very jolly and plucked each other's eyebrows. Then, just before daybreak, we were taken from our cell and hanged by our necks until we were dead. In my dream, death was Grey Paths Council Estate, stretching into infinity. Ruth and I set out to find the shopping centre. But . . .

I woke up at 6 a.m. and smelt burning meat. I dressed quickly in my Hartnell suit and plimsolls and went to investigate. Outside on the top landing the smell was stronger and was mixed with an acrid stench that stung the back of my throat. Looking down the stairs I saw wisps of smoke curling from under Keir's door.

'KEIR! KEIR! WAKE UP! THERE'S A FIRE IN YOUR ROOM!'

I banged on the door until my knuckles hurt. Letitia and Gerard came out of their room, lighting cigarettes. I shouted: 'Smoke!' and indicated the base of the door. The professor said: 'Perhaps the poor boy is hitting the ciggies more heavily than usual.' Letitia said: 'That's not fag smoke, dolt. Break the sodding door down!'

Eventually it was Letitia herself who shouldered the door aside, her husband having misjudged the angle and bounced off the architrave. Keir was sitting cross-legged on the floor, roasting a pigeon in the fireplace. A tiny coal fire glowed in the grate. Keir withdrew the toasting fork and poked at the pigeon's neck, testing it for edibility. He looked up at us dully. 'I hope you're not expecting to join me,' he said. 'There is no way this will stretch to four.'

'No sweat, old chap,' said Willoughby D'Eresby. 'Never did like pigeon, prefer woodcock.'

'Darling,' said Letitia, ruffling her son's matted hair, 'it *is* nice to see you eating. Shall I fetch you some redcurrant jelly?'

Keir spat out a feather and whined: 'I'm not eating because I want to *eat*. I'm doing this as a public service. If it wasn't for me, London would be overrun . . . They're vermin you know, absolutely crawling with parasites.'

'Yes, well, you will make sure it's cooked *through*, won't you, darling?' said Letitia, staring with some dismay at the pigeon's pin-button eyes. Keir turned his attention back to his cooking, and after a long pause the professor said, rather too heartily, 'Well, m'boy, we'll leave you to your breakfast.'

As we trooped out of the door Keir said: 'It isn't my breakfast, it's my *campaign*.' The only adult objects in Keir's room were the smoking materials on his bedside table. Even the toasting fork was stamped with Winnie the Pooh decorations. The room was a museum piece. There ought to have been a braided rope across the door and a printed card on the wall:

A TYPICAL FIVE-YEAR-OLD BOY'S BEDROOM
CIRCA 1969

'Is there much nourishment in a pigeon, darling?' asked Letitia outside Keir's door.

'There's protein of course,' replied Professor Willoughby D'Eresby. 'I'll have a word with Archie Duncan, the nutritionist.' And that was that. They went into the bathroom to share a bath.

I was reminded of a horror film I once saw. A group of holiday-makers had rented a Gothic castle for a fortnight. At dinner on the first night a violent thunderstorm broke out. A chandelier fell onto the dinner table. A statue toppled down the stairs. And all the candles went out and then mysteriously lit themselves again. Yet the holiday-makers cheerfully went to bed in their spooky bedrooms and managed to sleep through organ music and screams coming from the cellar.

The Willoughby D'Eresbys and the holiday-makers in the film had much in common: severe cases of taking life as it comes. Had Keir been born on the Grey Paths Estate he would have been secure in the care of the community. Some nosy neighbour would have reported him for strangling pigeons on the windowsill.

18 I Leave the Unconventional Household

I was stirring porridge when Professor Willoughby D'Eresby came into the kitchen and said, 'I've been watching breakfast television. Your name is Coventry Dakin, isn't it?'

'Yes.'

'Your photograph has just been on the news. In the photograph you're pointing some kind of firearm and looking quite fierce.'

'A firearm?' I was baffled.

'You look frightfully pretty in the photograph. You were wearing a rather fetching blue and white checked frock.'

'Oh *that*,' I said. 'It was a pop gun; the photograph was a joke. It was my son's birthday. . . .'

'According to the police you're rather dangerous. They have warned the public not to approach you.'

'Oh dear.'

'You have a grudge against men, according to the boys in blue.'

I shook my head.

'But you killed a man?'

'Yes.'

'So you are *rather* a violent person?'

The porridge was heaving about at the bottom of the pan, dangerously near to sticking. My wrist had gone limp; the wooden spoon bobbed about independently, rattling the sides of the saucepan.

'Are you going to turn me in?' I asked.

'Not *in*. But, sadly, *out*. It's not that I'm shocked, my dear. Murder is yawningly ordinary to me; but, even so, I cannot harbour you under my roof. I'm a professor of forensic medicine. I'm in daily contact with the police. You do see the position I'm in?'

'Yes.'

'Letitia is *desperately unhappy*. She was hoping that you'd be with us for years. Servants are such a problem, what with her naturism and Keir's eccentricities.'

'When do you want me to go?'

'I think immediately would be best, don't you? I'm so very sorry.'

The porridge burnt, so I gave them Weetabix. They ate in uncharacteristic silence. After I'd put the bowls in the dishwasher the Willoughby D'Eresbys gave me a leopard-skin coat and a fifty-pound note.

'Was it a *crime passionnel*?' asked Letitia. 'If so, you may be treated leniently by the courts.'

'What *is* a *crime passionnel*?'

The professor answered. 'It's French, m'dear. Means bumping off a person you've been rogering or want to roger. Usually because they've started rogering someone else. The frog judiciary recognize that when one's glands are overexcited, then one's common sense flies out of the window and one is likely to act somewhat erratically.'

I said, 'Oh no, it was nothing like that at all. There was never any question of . . . rogering.'

'Oh dear,' said Letitia. 'In that case I *shouldn't* give myself up; should you, Gerard?'

'Wife! Are you asking me to put myself in the place of a murderer? Have you forgotten that my profession *is* partly the investigation of murder?'

'I'm only asking you to empathize with the poor girl.'

'I do, I do. But you really mustn't ask for my advice on what I'd do or where I'd go should *I* have committed a murder.'

'But I didn't . . .'

'I expect I'd nip up to Scotland and plead sanctuary in my old friend Buffy's hilltop castle. He's got twenty thousand acres of low-lying ground for a garden . . . and a moat. Could see the boys in blue approaching for three miles. Simple, pull up the drawbridge, pretend we've all gone to the shops and sit in front of the library fire with a Trollope and a glass of Scotland's finest. There, Letitia, are you satisfied? That's what I would do. Good old Buffy, decent old stick.'

'Husband, shut your gob. Coventry doesn't want to hear about that dreadful snuff-stained old soak you call a friend. She's anxious to be off, aren't you, dear?'

I shook their hands. Then they both kissed me and I opened the door and left. The professor came out onto the steps to wave me goodbye, but Letitia, being naked, stayed inside the house and waved through the letter-box.

The late autumn sun was showing off like mad, getting in people's eyes, dazzling drivers, illuminating dirty windows. I sweated inside the leopard-skin coat. The trees in Russell Square gardens flamed red in the buoyant air as I threw two pound-coins onto the patch of grass where I'd lain, underneath Leslie, the man with the missing teeth.

There was a little café in the corner of the gardens. A sprinkling of chairs and tables were set outside. It didn't seem like England, more like how I imagined a Saturday abroad to be. I ordered a cup of coffee and a toasted teacake, then remembered I'd only got a fifty-pound note.

'I don't suppose you can change . . . ?' I held the large note out.

'You suppose right, lady. This ain't the tea-room at the Ritz. I ain't catering for the moneyed classes 'ere.'

I went back to the area where I'd tossed the two pound-coins, found them, picked one up, left the other, went back to the café and paid the man behind the counter.

He laughed. 'Christ, lady, you got a good nose for money, ain't you? . . . Just leaps from the grass into your hands.'

It felt very strange to be sitting in the sunlight, smoking a cigarette and drinking my coffee, with nowhere to go and nothing to do. No husband hurrying me to drink up and move on. No whining children rocking the table and spilling their Coca Cola. I think the strange feeling was happiness.

Whenever Gerald Fox's dead face swam into my mind, I pushed it out.

It was only ten-thirty in the morning, so the whole day stretched ahead. My agenda was that of a rich woman: buy shoes, get ears pierced, find a hotel room. But meanwhile, how lovely to sit under the trees and look around. I left when the sun went in. The man behind the counter shouted: 'See you, your ladyship,' as I fastened my fur coat around me and left the gardens.

19 Boots to Change My Life

'Into fifties stuff, are you?' said the girl in the shoe shop.

'Fifties what?'

'*Fifties*, as in nineteen-fifties,' she said, looking at my suit and coat. 'You want some roach killers like these?' she said, showing me a pair of spiky stilettos with pointed toes.

'Winkle-pickers,' I said. 'We used to call them winkle-pickers in my day.'

'When was your day?' she asked.

'Nineteen fifty-seven,' I said.

'Oh, so you're not into fifties *nostalgia*, then?'

'No, I'm the real thing. Could I see a pair of comfortable ankle boots, please? Something I can run in?'

I love my boots. I keep looking at them and feeling the soft leather. I like the way the laces bind them tight around my feet and ankles. I could run ten miles, dance a ballet or climb a rock face in them.

'I want to wear them now,' I said to the girl. She took my fifty-pound note and my old plimsolls and gave me back thirty pounds, one penny and a carrier bag, which contained my disgraceful old shoes. The boots are so soft that they have already taken on the shape of my feet. I can see every one of my toes, and the slight bunion on each foot. I love my boots. I intend to buy them a tube of black polish. These boots are going to keep me out of prison, find me a job and change my life.

20 Sidney Comes Up for a Breath

'Ruth?'

'Yes.'

'It's Coventry!'

'Oh hello, Cov, how are you?'

'I'm very well, how are you?'

'I've had a bad tummy, due to a dubious chicken, but I'm all right now. How's Derek and the kids?'

'I don't know.'

'Why not?'

'I'm not at home, am I?'

'Aren't you?'

'No, I'm in London. Hasn't Sidney told you?'

'Told me what?'

'I'm in a bit of trouble.'

'Shoplifting?'

'No. He didn't tell you?'

'You've left Derek?'

'I can't believe he didn't tell you.'

'You've got cancer; you're in hospital.'

'No.'

'You've run off with another man?'

'No.'

Ruth sighed. 'Look, I'll fetch Sidney. He's in the pool with his snorkel gear, so I may have to wait for him to come up for a breath.'

'I'm in a phone box, Ruth. Hurry.'

I had put three pounds of my precious money into the slot before Sidney came to the phone.

'Cov? Sorry, couldn't find my fags.'

'Hello, Sidney.'

'Look, Cov, I told you to give me a week.'

'I'm frightened. I was passing the phone box and I had all these fifty-pence pieces. I bought some boots and she gave me five pounds' worth of silver.'

'Look, stop crying; you know it upsets me.'

'Why didn't you tell Ruth?'

'Because I want to enjoy myself, Cov. I'm not spending the rest of my holiday sitting at the side of the pool watching Ruth break out in eczema. She's already a bloody nervous wreck due to the Portuguese drivers. You should see the mad buggers; talk about "see the Algarve and die".'

'When will you be back in England, *exactly*?'

'Sunday afternoon. Gatwick. Give me a bell at the shop on Monday, eh?'

'I've got no more money to put in.'

'Keep your pecker up, Cov.'

'Yes and yours.'

'Mine's always up.'

He laughed and put the phone down.

I shouldn't have made the phone call; it was a mad extravagance. My only excuse is that I love my brother and I wanted to hear his voice. Had Sidney murdered somebody and needed my help, I would have walked across Portugal and France and swum whichever sea separated us. I would give Sidney my last penny. I would lie and cheat and steal and fight to protect him from unhappiness. It is a great sadness to me that Sidney does not love me with the same intensity.

I've got twenty-five pounds and a penny in a pocket of the leopard-skin coat. I am usually very careful with money. I know *exactly* where every penny goes. Went. Derek opted to receive a wage packet every week rather than have his wages paid into the bank, like most of the shop floor workers. Every Friday night he and I would sit at the kitchen table and divide the money into little piles. Derek clicked on his calculator and instructed me what to put where. Then I would note down the figures in a red cash book. The total could never exceed eighty-one pounds, sixty-seven pence which was Derek's net weekly earnings. If I say it myself, I was an excellent housekeeper. I was very clever with offal. Everything that came into the house that was usable was washed and recycled. It was a full-time occupation. I knew the prices in the supermarket by heart. I took note of seasonal fluctuations. I bought sheets and pillowcases in the January sales, mended my own shoes, knitted, sewed and crocheted our clothes. I made birthday and Christmas cards (including envelopes), bread, cakes and biscuits. We grew our own vegetables and flowers, cut our own hair. When we were ill we waited until we were better. There was no column in the red cash book for prescriptions. We were careful with light and heat. The central heating was never turned on before mid-October, and it was turned off religiously on Good Friday. Derek cycled to work with a box of sandwiches in his saddle bag. There was an egg-timer by the phone.

We had no credit cards or charge accounts. Derek's subscription to the Tortoise Society was only four pounds a year (including the bi-annual newsletter). I wore little make-up, used no hairspray. Our video was a present from my mother, who had given up trying to work out how to use it. Derek made most of our furniture; consequently there was hardly anything in the house that didn't rock, tilt or stick.

Our last holiday was a coach tour of Scotland five years ago. Both children were travel-sick, and when we were all bitten by midges there was no spare money with which to buy antihistamine cream. We had to cadge squirts from the pensioners who made up the rest of the coach party.

In our house money was a god. But it was an angry, careful god. It wasn't a question of worshipping money, but fearing it. Consequently we lived timid lives; only the financially secure can afford to be spontaneous.

'If only the children would stop *growing*,' Derek would say. Because, of course, it was the children who sapped our monetary strength. Without certain *things* they could not live. To Derek and me it was inconceivable that our children would not be happy. We had both been unhappy children, you see. That's why we got married; to reproduce ourselves and have another stab at happiness.

Instead of being sensible and finding a cheap hotel, I had my ears pierced in Regent Street. I was surprised at how much it hurt. The girl with the stud gun told me that it was strictly against the rules to remove the little gold studs she'd inserted. Also, I must rotate them every four hours and clean my lobes with white spirit, unless I wanted a 'major infection of the ears'. She then lectured me on wild life preservation. I explained that the leopard-skin coat was a gift, but she told me that it was 'the principle that counted'. She said this as if it were the first time it had been said. 'I don't know how you can bear to walk around with a dead animal on your back,' she said, as she creaked about in her leather suit. While we waited for my ears to stop bleeding, I agreed that it was a callous thing to do, which pleased the girl. An expression of my mother's escaped out of my mouth before I could stop it: 'Needs must.'

'What does that mean?'

'It means I've got nothing else to keep me warm,' I said.

As soon as I got outside the shop I took the studs out and put the jade earrings in. Letitia was right, they look lovely with my orange hair. I am now down to fifteen pounds and one penny; and I'm going to be sensible and start looking for a hotel room.

21 John Goes to Bradford

John Dakin and Bradford Keynes faced each other over the easels in the art room of the Workers' Educational Institute. They were surrounded by grey and balding heads, as pensioners bent over their Titian copies.

'I've come about my mum.'

'Who is your mum?'

'Lauren McSkye,' lied John.

Bradford's heart tingled with a thousand electric shocks. He forgot to breathe. The blood fled from beneath his skin. He was knocked off balance. He was twenty-six.

'Do you know where she is?' asked John, wondering to himself if this scruff with paint on his long, ridiculous beard was drunk in the middle of the day.

Bradford had fallen violently in love with Lauren McSkye within three minutes of their first meeting in January. Since then he only lived so that he might look at her and listen to her voice. In between their twice weekly innocent meetings he was bereft; during the night he painted feverishly: Lauren in her black outfit, Lauren naked, Lauren . . . Lauren . . . Lauren.

'No, I don't know where she is.' Bradford's voice wobbled out of control. 'She's missed two lessons. She wouldn't ever give an address, so I didn't know where to *begin* to look for her.'

There was an obsessional tone to his voice. John put it down to Bradford being an artist; everybody knew they were loonies, always cutting their ears off or running away from respectable jobs to live on islands with a load of savages. 'She left her work here,' said Bradford, who was anxious to detain Lauren's son for as long as possible. He needed more information about Lauren so that he could suck on it and chew it and digest it, when he got back to his dingy terraced house. Bradford held up a picture.

John looked contemptuously at his mother's daubing. 'A kid could do better,' he thought.

Bradford looked at the same painting. 'A true primitive,' he thought, 'true and fine and innocent.'

Lauren McSkye/Coventry Dakin had painted, at Bradford's request, 'Heaven'. There was a river with a slow-running current, boats were being rowed both up and down stream. The banks of the river were stocked with fruit trees and oaks. Weeping willows languished in the water. Geraniums, daffodils, foxgloves and buttercups and daisies tumbled down the river banks. A woman who looked like Lauren lay back against a pile of jewelled cushions. She was reading a book. A box of Black Magic chocolates lay on the verdant grass. Bottles of wine and an Edam cheese could be seen in the raffia basket at her feet. The sun and the moon and the stars were out together in the sky. There was only one cloud to be seen. In the far distance were a town, a mountain, a sea, a lighthouse and a sign which said in tiny lettering: 'At last, full employment, minimum wage £200 a week.'

'Did you know your mother could paint?' asked Bradford.

'No,' said John. He thought, 'She *can't* paint: it's crap.'

'Is your mother not at home, then?' said Bradford.

'No, she's gone off somewhere.'

'I see. I didn't realize your mother had children. Is she married?'

'Yes, to my dad. Derek McSkye.'

'I see, and your name is . . . ?'

'John McSkye. I've got a sister, Mary McSkye.'

'Is your father an American?'

'No.'

'Oh; your mother's accent . . . where do you live?'

'Not far from here.'

'Exactly where?'

Bradford had searched the telephone book in vain. There were no McSkyes.

'I've gotta go to college now.' John swung the strap of his canvas bag onto his shoulder. Bradford saw that the bag was clearly marked in indelible ink:

THE PROPERTY OF JOHN DAKIN
13, BADGER'S COPSE CLOSE
GREY PATHS ESTATE

The ink had smudged, but the address still made an indelible impression on Bradford Keynes. There was no need for him to write it down.

22 Cardboard City

Have you heard of Cardboard City? It's where I live.

It is within sight of Waterloo Station and a mere bottle's throw from the River Thames. In other circumstances it would make an ideal *pied à terre* but, as it is, it lacks certain facilities such as: a roof, walls, windows, a floor, hot and cold water, a lavatory, a bath, electricity, gas, a front door. There are no houses in Cardboard City, only homes, which have been constructed on the DIY principle from the detritus of other people's lives. Cardboard is used, of course, and plastic sheeting, and anything else that will keep the cold out and the body heat in. The residents of Cardboard City are unusually well informed; they are great newspaper readers. The larger, quality newspapers are preferred, as they have superior insulating factors.

Nobody asks questions in Cardboard City; information is either volunteered or not given at all. Sometimes stories told drunkenly late at night are retracted in the sober light of morning. The only thing the residents have in common is their poverty and their will to survive. Perhaps one more thing: the inability to manage money. This is why *I'm* here, after all. If I'd taken a cheap hotel room instead of eating three meals a day, then perhaps I could have found a job; but without an address nobody would employ me.

Then, when my photograph appeared in the national papers, I had to hide. I spent my last money on a pair of Woolworth's sun-glasses. I wear them day and night. Several people have helped me to cross busy road junctions, thinking that I am blind or partially-sighted. I've been sleeping here for three days. I've got a posh friend called Dodo. She's exactly one month older than me. We protect each other. The other residents are sometimes inclined towards noisy – and violent – confrontations.

Dodo is teaching me survival techniques. We are living off the thin of the land; but at least we're engaged in living. Some time ago Dodo had a nervous breakdown. She *used* to think that she was the chief constable of Manchester; God told her she was, and she believed God and went to Manchester Police HQ and asked for a fitting for a chief constable's uniform. Naturally she was thrown out, but she went back, twice a day for a fortnight, and eventually the police got fed up with her and put her away in a safe place.

Dodo liked the mental hospital. 'You could be as mad as you liked,' she said. 'And it was warm and safe, and there were lovely grounds to stroll about in when the weather was fine.'

The problems came when Dodo got slightly better – when God stopped talking to her. The doctors decided that Dodo was well enough to live in the community. She was sent to a halfway house, and made to live with five other half-mad people. One of the five was an arsonist who had a penchant for burning down hotels. He was not allowed matches or cigarette lighters or combustibles of any kind and he was given weekly support from his social worker but, ungratefully, some would say, he still managed to set fire to the halfway house. A neighbour who had signed a petition against having the hostel in the street woke the other residents and helped them to safety. As he did so, he composed a letter in his mind: it was to the local paper:

'Dear Sir, Entirely as I predicted . . .'

Instead of being sensible and reporting for a roll call, Dodo warmed her hands on the flames, and then ran away. The firemen searched the gutted wreck in the morning, looking for her burnt body.

According to Dodo she comes from a well-known political family. She *says* that her brother is the former – now disgraced – Cabinet Minister, Nicholas Cutbush. I don't believe a word of this. It's just another variation on her wanting to be chief constable of Manchester.

At night Dodo and I cling together like passionate spoons. We need the warmth and the *warmth*. Our present little house is made out of two fridge-freezer boxes and is well insulated with polystyrene blocks; the pavements are cruelly cold in London. During the day, when we are out begging, a fellow resident of Cardboard City, called James Spittlehouse, guards our cardboard shelter. In return for this kindness Dodo and I lay scraps of food at his feet. Mr Spittlehouse has an unpredictable temperament and a terrible criminal record. He has over a hundred convictions for stealing from church poor-boxes. 'Well, I *am* poor,' he says defiantly. 'It cuts out the middleman, saves all them committee meetings. They don't have to decide how to hand the money out, do they? 'Cause *I've* already had it.' He speaks longingly of the cosy cells and companionship of prison. He even misses slopping out. His proudest boast is that he is a virgin.

'I've never been touched by man, woman or beast. The last person to touch my secret parts was my own mother, and even then a sponge intervened.'

Mr Spittlehouse disapproves of fraternization between the sexes. He wears four pairs of underpants in case a passing woman should be tempted to interfere with him. Dodo and I have tried to reassure him on this point, but he won't be told.

The police turn a blind eye to Cardboard City; there are too many of us and there is nowhere else for us to go. We are an embarrassment. Commuters passing to and fro to the trains at Waterloo hate us. They hate us so much that they cannot look at us. If one of us falls in their path (and there are many drunks amongst us), the commuters step over the body and carry on walking. They hate us because we have time. We are rich with time, we are overflowing with it and they are short of it, always.

Gerald Fox has been dead one week today.

23 Homo Impecunious Working Class

Professor Willoughby D'Eresby looked up from the report on Gerald Fox's autopsy.

Letitia said, 'Well, come on, you old bleeder, cough it up. Spill the beans; what does it *say*?'

'It says "Massive Cerebral Haemorrhage".'

'Caused by an Action Man?' scoffed Letitia.

'Yes. I note the doubt in your voice, wife.'

'It's sodding ridiculous. Who did the autopsy?'

'Roger Skillet. Knew him at Oxford. He was a lazy sod then, and I doubt if thirty-odd years in the provinces have improved his deductive skills. Still, it was good of him to send me the papers.'

Letitia had left her office in Tavistock Square at lunch-time the day before and tried to buy an Action Man doll. However the sales assistant informed her that Action Man was no longer manufactured, so Letitia rang around her non-pacifist friends who still had young children. Eventually she tracked Action Man down. He was now sitting amongst the debris and clutter on the kitchen table. His little beret was tipped at a jaunty angle over his serious pink face. His hands were crossed modestly over his asexual groin. Letitia had, in the name of forensic science, removed his tiny camouflage uniform and Tom Thumb army boots.

'He's quite sweet, isn't he, husband?' Letitia picked up the naked doll and waggled its legs about. She spoke to it. '*You* wouldn't kill a big man would you, sweetie? No, of course you wouldn't. You're too itsy-bitsy, aren't you?' She turned to her husband.

'Is Fox's body around?'

'Yes, he's still in cold storage. Apparently his liver is of great interest to the Alcohol Abuse boys. In fact, reading his report, I wonder how Fox actually managed to function at all. Dreadful condition for a man in his late thirties: lungs shot to hell, varicose veins, piles, furred up arteries, hammer toes, thin skull, pea brain, brittle bones, dandruff, clogged up sinuses, polyps up his nose, athlete's foot, overweight, pyorrhoea, ingrowing toenails . . . small

95

contusion at the base of the skull, caused by our Action Man friend but no real damage. I don't think our Coventry did kill Mr Fox, Letitia. I think he probably killed himself. Apoplexy! . . . Heartsome news, eh?'

Letitia hit her husband playfully on the back of the neck with the little naked soldier. 'Would you have bothered with all this if Coventry had been as ugly as sin, husband?'

'Probably not, wife,' admitted W.D.

24 Derek Wipes the Surfaces

One afternoon after work, Derek Dakin saw the widow Carole Fox open the door of her council house and shepherd her four little daughters inside. 'Plucky little thing,' he thought. 'I must go over and give her my condolences.' Eight days had passed since her cruel bereavement. Derek went to the bookcase and looked up 'condolences' in a Victorian etiquette book, *Manners and Rules of Good Society by a Member of the Aristocracy*, but there was nothing in it about the correct procedure in which a meeting could take place between the husband of a murderess and the widow of her victim.

'Play it by ear,' thought Derek, and he left his house and crossed the road and knocked on No 12. Four-year-old Kirsty Fox opened the door.

'Is your mummy there?'

'Yes, she's on the toilet.'

Derek told Kirsty that he would wait on the doorstep. A chain pulled upstairs, water flushed and Carole Fox clumped down the narrow stairs. When she saw Derek she flinched back as though Derek were about to fly at her with clenched fists.

'You frit me to death,' she said.

Derek winced; her local accent was very pronounced. Derek had almost succeeded in eradicating his.

'Mrs Fox, I'd just like to say how very sorry I am about . . .'

'S'all right.'

'You must be devastated.'

'What?'

'Devastated.'

'What?'

'*Devastated*.'

Carole nodded, thinking that it would get rid of him quicker if she agreed.

'How have the little girls taken it?'

She lowered her voice. 'I an't told 'em yet, they think he's on 'is 'olidays – in Penzance.'

'Oh, but didn't they watch . . . ? See? Weren't they exposed to the sight of . . . ? What happened . . . ?'

'Oh yeah, they *seen* it, but they din't know 'e was *dead*. They was used to seein' 'im lying about on the floor with 'is eyes closed. 'E was an 'eavy drinker, y'know.'

'And how are *you?*'

'Who me? Oh, I'm all right; it's peaceful without 'im. Your wife done me a favour. He wudda done *me* in before long. I 'ated 'im.'

'Could I step inside for a moment, Mrs Fox?'

'Well, I've not 'ad a chance to clean up yet today,' said Carole, as though Derek were an inspector from the Ministry of Clean Houses.

'There's something I must know.'

'All right.'

Carole led the way into the living-room, kicking articles of clothing aside as she went. The little Fox girls were sitting on the floor eating bowls of cornflakes. The television was showing close-ups of open-heart surgery. Afternoon viewing. Carole and Derek sat at a table at the far end of the room. Derek looked out at the Fox garden – a brown and grey plot of earth which contained no living plant. Wrecked dolls' prams constituted the only border.

'Do you read a daily paper, Mrs Fox?'

'Who me? No, 'e used to, but I've got me 'ands full with the kids.'

Derek mentioned to Carole that the popular press were suggesting that her dead husband and Coventry had been having an affair. Did Carole know anything about these suppositions?

'Who me? As I say, I've got me 'ands full. He went out every night but . . . they say the wife's the last to know, don't they?' Carole's eyes flicked to the television and she watched throbbing arteries until Derek spoke again.

'I'd like to do something for you, Mrs Fox.'

'Who me? What kind of thing?'

'Dig the garden . . . shelves . . . I'm very good with my hands. And you'll need a man about the house *now*, won't you?'

'Who me? Why? I never 'ad one *before.*'

'Are you all right financially?'

'Money?'

'Yes.'

'I'm *better* off, now. I've got me social sorted. We're better off all round, really.'

Derek felt slightly cheated. There was a mini-packet of tissues in his trouser pocket. He had expected to whip them out for the moment when the grieving widow broke down. Mrs Fox's perspicuity unsettled him. He decided she was in shock, deep shock. They watched in companionable silence as a surgeon's lackey stitched up the chest cavity and made everything neat and tidy for the patient. When the programme ended Derek went into the poorly equipped kitchen and made Carole and himself a nice cup of tea. Then he tackled the washing-up and wiped the surfaces down. It was the least he could do.

25 The Widowing of Dodo

Nobody in Cardboard City, not even the stupefied alcoholics, manages to get a healthy eight hours' sleep. Dodo and I settle in our box at midnight but we usually wake at three o'clock. There is nothing else to do then but share a careful cigarette and talk.

Dodo told me how she was widowed three years ago. 'Geoffrey and I were driving back from the country; we'd been staying with Tobias Marrows-Callandine . . . lovely house . . . listed Grade Two. Georgian or Saxon or something. Sixteen unheated bedrooms, *foul* dog, wonderful lake – anyway we were tootling along in the Porsche; I was driving, *very carefully*, over the Hammersmith Flyover. We were laughing rather hysterically about the weekend: poor old Marrows-Callandine had claimed that his wife was ill and couldn't get out of bed and do all the hostessing and stuff. Naturally I volunteered to go up and take her a tray – that sort of thing. Marrows-Callandine turned me down, very emphatic he was. Said his wife had expressed the wish to be completely ignored over the weekend. This was on Friday night, anyway, where was I? . . . Yes . . . By Sunday morning I'm desperately searching the bloody house for a fan heater. I ask you, middle of winter and *one* log fire in the entire house. I go into this dark bedroom, put the light on and see Lucia Marrows-Callandine lying in bed. She has two black eyes, a broken nose and four missing teeth. Poor cow starts to whimper, says she loves Tobias and forgives him; and could I bring her a Mars bar or something because she hasn't eaten for a day and a half.

'Of course I tackle Tobias on this and he says, "Poor Lucia, she had a tantrum on Friday morning, dishwasher overflowed or something, and *she beat herself up.*"

'So Geoffrey and I were laughing at what the bullying turd had said. Then Geoff reaches over into the back and picks up a bottle of Coca Cola. He lifts it to his mouth, a cat runs in front of the car, I brake and the Coca Cola rams down the back of Geoff's throat, blood everywhere.

'Geoff died. Didn't take long. My mother's such a snob. I rang her from the hospital to tell her the news. She said, "Coca Cola? My God, will it be in the papers? Couldn't you say it was Malvern Water?" '

With such stories we keep ourselves interested, though not always amused. I have told Dodo nearly everything about myself – except my name and the fact that I am a murderer.

26 Carole Fox's Evidence

CAROLE: It were about five o'clock. I'd just put the lights on in the living-room.

CORONER: The room that faced the street?

CAROLE: Yes. I heard him come in. I could tell by the way he opened the front door that he was in one of his moods. Then I heard 'im goin' mad 'cos the doormat had got caught under the door. Anyway he come in the living-room and he'd been drinking.

CORONER: How did you know he'd been drinking?

CAROLE: Because he was drunk.

CORONER: Thank you. Carry on, Mrs Fox.

CAROLE: Well, the girls got out his way. They're not daft – they knew there'd be trouble; and he walked round the room a bit, finding fault, like he always did. He shouted at me because the clock had stopped. Then he had a go because the kids' toys were still on the floor. Then he started going on about Jennifer, she's seven, saying that she wasn't 'is. She's got red hair, you see. The others are dark, like him. Then he got proper worked up and said *none* of the girls was 'is, 'cos none of 'em 'ad 'is nose; and he said that I'd got to write down the names of all the men I'd been with.

CORONER: By 'been with', I assume your husband meant – men that you'd slept with?

CAROLE: No, I didn't sleep with any . . .

CORONER: No, I'm sure you . . . carry on.

CAROLE: He fetched some Basildon Bond I'd had for Christmas, and a pen from the sideboard, and he pushed me down on the settee and told me to write the names of these men. All the time he was shouting about how I was a slag, and he knew I slept with the meter readers who came to the 'ouse.

CORONER: And your daughters were still in the room at the time?

CAROLE: Yes, they were in the corner, near the telly. They were too frit to move or owt. Anyroad I were makin' up men's names and writing them down. To tell the truth I were between the devil and the deep blue sea. If I *didn't* write owt he'd give me one for not doin' as I was told, and if I *did* . . .

CORONER: Would you like a moment . . . a glass of water . . . a tissue?

CAROLE: No, I'm all right. Sorry, I've gotta 'anky. He were goin' mad, shouting as how he'd go round and beat the . . . sorry, he said a swear word . . . out of anybody on the list. He said I wasn't fit to bear the fine name of Fox and that I'd dragged him down and it were my fault he'd never got on in life. His face were like a beetroot and his eyes was bulging out is 'ead. I could see the veins in his neck all sticking out and sort of throbbing. I thought, 'Oh God, Carole, 'e's goin' to kill you!' Normally, when he's, like, in one of 'is moods 'e chucks stuff about . . .

CORONER: You mean he throws objects?

CAROLE: He throws owt. I've 'ad more than *objects* thrown at me . . . anyroad this time 'e didn't. So I knew I were really gonna get it; 'an I did. 'E started kicking me legs while I were sittin' down. Then 'e pulled me up by me 'air and started punchin' me face. The girls, the girls . . . they . . . well they . . .

CORONER: When you're ready, Mrs Fox. Please, take as long as you need.

CAROLE: Well the girls, they were cryin' and sayin', 'Daddy don't' and things like that. Then he got me by the throat. He were like somebody on the telly; he'd gone mad. He were chokin' me and screamin' at me. Then Coventry from over the road come in and 'it 'im with the Action Man and he dropped down straight away, and blood came out of 'is ears.

CORONER: Did Coventry, that is Coventry Dakin, say anything before or after she hit your husband?

CAROLE: She said sommat like, 'I've had enough of you' before she 'it 'im; and after she 'it 'im she said nowt. She just run out and nobody's seen her since. Well, nobody round 'ere 'as.

CORONER: Mrs Dakin lived opposite you?

CAROLE: Yes, at Number 13.

CORONER: Your curtains were not drawn?

CAROLE: I 'adn't drawn 'em, no.

CORONER: So Mrs Dakin was able to watch the events prior to your husband's death?

CAROLE: I don't know, sorry. Could you say it again . . . ?

CORONER: Mrs Dakin saw your husband beating you up?

CAROLE: She must have. She 'adn't drawn 'er own livin'-room

curtains. It's not the first time she's seen 'im have a go at me.

CORONER: Mrs Fox, you said your husband dropped down straight away and blood came out of his ears. Did blood *immediately* come out of his ears or did some time pass before you saw the blood? Think carefully, please.

CAROLE: It come out as soon as 'is 'ead 'it the carpet. Some splashed out on me zebra-skin rug in front of the fire. 'Is 'ead bounced, you see, and the blood come out.

CORONER: Thank you, Mrs Fox. You have been an excellent witness. You have the jury's sympathy and mine.

CAROLE: Thank you. If it wasn't for Coventry I think it might have been *me* lying dead, instead of 'im. She done me a favour.

CORONER: The jury will disregard those last remarks. Thank you, Mrs Fox.

CAROLE: Sorry. Thank you, your Honour . . . sorry, Mr Coroner. Shall I go back to where I was sittin' before?

27 Saturday Morning on the Algarve

Sidney and Ruth's sweaty bodies made a loud slurping sound as they separated from each other, like trifle being lifted from a dish. Ruth blushed and hid her face under the damp sheet. Sidney lit a cigarette then lay on his back, with a Portuguese folk art ashtray balancing on his damp belly. It was the last opportunity they would have for leisurely morning sex. Tomorrow morning they would have to be up and packed and getting into the car for the hazardous drive to the airport.

The bedside telephone rang. Sidney knew that this meant trouble, so he let it ring. On and on and on and on. Ruth stuffed her head under a pillow.

'Sidney, please.'

'No, let it ring.'

'It might be my mum.'

'It won't be, I gave her the wrong number.'

'Deliberately?'

'Yes.'

'You're awful, you are. You really are, Sidney.'

Sidney admired his wife's body as she got up from the bed and padded around on the tiled floor, looking for her kimono. The telephone continued to ring.

'Sidney, answer it, it's hurting my ears!'

'No. Jesus, you've got a fantastic tan, Ruth. Your back's the colour of Marmite toast. No, don't put any clothes on yet, I want to look at you.'

'You've done nothing but look at me for a fortnight. It's creepy. Sometimes you give me the creeps. You're never satisfied. You're not normal, Sidney. I mean it's not as if I'm nice to look at, is it? . . . ANSWER THE PHONE!'

'No, come back to bed.'

'No.'

'No?'

'Yes. No!'

Ruth had played submission games in the past. Once or twice she had even enjoyed them, but now, with the telephone ringing and with the aquarium smell of sex still on her, she was not playing. She meant 'NO'. She walked out of the bedroom and into the shuttered living-room where she answered the other, more ornate telephone.

'Hello?'

'Mrs Lambert? Mrs Ruth Lambert?'

'Yes.'

'This is Detective Inspector Sly, Mrs Lambert. I was just wondering if you've heard anything from your sister-in-law, Coventry?'

'Yes, she phoned in the week. Are you a policeman?'

'Did she say where she was?'

'Yes, London. Has she had an accident?'

'Is your husband there, Mrs Lambert?'

'Yes.'

'Could I have a word with him?'

Sidney was still lying on the bed. He was holding a hand mirror up to the underside of his erection.

'Sidney! For God's sake, what are you *doing*?'

'I was just checking for testicular cancer.'

'Don't tell lies Sidney, you were *admiring* yourself. Nobody smiles like that when they're checking for cancer. You're wanted on the phone; it's a policeman . . . something about Coventry.'

Sidney lifted the receiver from the phone by the bed.

'Sidney Lambert speaking.'

'Detective Inspector Sly here, sir. Truscott Road police station. According to your wife, you've been withholding information from me. When are you back in England?'

'Sunday afternoon, late,' said Sidney. His erection rapidly subsided.

He also put the phone down.

28 How the Other Half Live

Dodo wants to go home and collect some clothes. She wants me to go with her. Home is where her brother lives in London. We will have to be careful because Dodo thinks she is wanted by the authorities. She lacks a signed bit of paper saying that she is perfectly sane. I have always feared authority. I am a pedestrian, yet I'm scared of traffic wardens. I don't know why this should be.

We are going out begging this morning; Dodo says that Saturday is always a good day. In the afternoon we intend to rebuild our cardboard house, and then, in darkness, we are going to Flood Street, where Nicholas Cutbush lives with his wife. There are no Cutbush children; Nicholas has got unreliable genes and his wife has a career.

This is how we beg. We always approach women of our own age and Dodo's class. We prefer harassed-looking women carrying shopping bags. They are not hard to find. We stand outside an exclusive department store (when I was a child I thought you had to be a *member* to get inside the only such shop in my home town). Dodo and I always carry Harrods carrier bags. We sleep on them at night to iron out the creases in the plastic. When we see a sufficiently harassed woman, we go into action. Dodo bursts into tears and shouts out in an anguished way, 'Oh my God, it had everything inside it – my purse, my Filofax, my prescriptions, my insulin,' then, when the harassed woman's attention is gained (nine times out of ten), 'Oh no! Oh no! . . . The children's baby pictures!'

My role is to comfort Dodo, ask for the woman's help and then, when the woman has been drawn into the drama, to gasp and say, 'Dodo, *my purse*, remember? I asked you to put it in your handbag. Now we can't even afford a *taxi*.' Dodo then has to break out into fresh weeping (she's astonishingly good at this). Most of our harassed women cough up the taxi fare without being directly asked. The average payment is two pounds. Do these women think we could get *anywhere* for two pounds?

So far the most we have begged in a day is twenty-eight pounds.

We, of course, split this between us. With my half I bought thermal underwear and socks. Dodo blew hers on a bottle of vodka and Belgian chocolates from Liberty's. I know this can't go on for ever. I don't want to live like this.

Dodo says, 'Darling, we're doing *them* a service. Think how pleased they are at being able to help two temporarily destitute women. And it's an anecdote for them, isn't it? Something to talk about to their oaf.'

Dodo calls all men 'oafs'; she doesn't like them much. I do, though . . . just about.

We strolled along the embankment, until it got dark and the river was only a reflection from the lighted buildings; then we set out for Flood Street. We walk everywhere. Dodo likes pointing out interesting buildings and landmarks. I already know which bridge is which. Tonight we crossed Westminster Bridge and I made Dodo stop while I had a good look up and down at the river. Dodo called me a 'provincial' but she looked at the views and said, 'Good old London,' before we walked on. It took us an hour to reach Flood Street. I was disappointed. I'd expected bigger houses. Hadn't Dodo said her brother was once a Cabinet Minister? Or did she say cabinet maker?

A car drew up outside a house and a chauffeur got out and opened a rear door. A tall, dark man got out. He was carrying a very large bouquet of dusky red roses.

'That's Nick,' said Dodo. 'Looks like he's been asset stripping Interflora.' The car purred off and Dodo ran up to her brother. 'Nick!' He leapt away from her and scrambled his key in the lock of the shiny black front door.

'Not tonight, Dodo. We've got *people* in and I'm late.'

'I only want some clothes. This is my friend.' We stood on the threshold, our feet just inside the door like successful Jehovah's Witnesses.

'It's Caroline's *birthday*, Dodo, we're having a *dinner party*.'

'Then I would like to wish her a happy birthday, Nick. Please let me in.'

'Dodo, you're a complete *cow*.'

'Bastard.'

'Bitch.'

A tall, thin woman in a rustling dress had joined us.

108

'Neck? Is that you, Neck? What's that with you?'

'Hello, Caro. Dodo, fuck off. *Fuck off, Dodo!*'

'Oh Dodo, is that really you, darling?'

'Yes. It's fucking Dodo, come to spoil the fun. Oh, these are for you, darling. Happy birthday!'

'Thanks. Dodo, how well you look! Are you still living raff? Come in and shut the door. Who's this, a friend?'

'Yes, we share a box. I call her Jaffa – because of her hair.'

'How do you do, Jaffa. I'm Caroline. I think you've met my husband.'

We were crammed into the tiny hall. At the end of the passage a door was slightly ajar. I could see a twinkling chandelier, candles, silver, linen and half of an off-the-shoulder dress. I could hear crystal accents and comfortable laughter. I could smell food and a coal fire and flowers. A classical tune reminded me of 'Family Favourites' and Cliff Michelmore.

The door at the end of the passage opened and a famous face appeared. He was not a celebrity; he didn't appear on panel games; but he was on television most nights of the week. He was something to do with the government, the law, the police . . . the Home Office. He looked delighted to see Dodo.

'Well beggar me, if it isn't Dodo! We were only jest talking about you. Caroline tells me you're now sane.'

'Oh quite. You're looking awful, Podger.'

'It's the new job; blame your brother. If he hadn't got his tits caught in the mangle, I'd still be slumbering away in Ag and Fish.'

'Yes, I'm sorry you lost your job, Nick,' said Dodo.

We were now walking down the hall towards the twinkling room. Nick said, 'My own stupid fault for taking an MI5 file into Groucho's.'

'No, dear old son, the stupid thing was *leaving* it there for Ian Hislop to find.'

There was much merry laughter, which took us into the dining-room.

'Dodo!' shouted four well-dressed people at once. There was a scramble to embrace her. Nick stood aside, sulking. When she emerged from the crowd, Dodo introduced me to the company.

'This is Jaffa, we share the same cardboard box.' More laughter. I shook everyone's soft hands, then was taken away by Caroline to freshen up. Dodo stayed downstairs to gossip with her friends.

Caroline's clothes were hung around the walls of two rooms. She told me to hurry up and pick something, anything I liked. In the background a bathtub was filling up with perfumed bubbles.

I chose a green satin strapless evening dress, which had a stiff flounced skirt and a dozen net petticoats. Each one a different shade of green, like Irish counties.

'How old are you?' asked Caroline, when I was bathed and dressed and brushing my hair.

'I'm forty tomorrow,' I said.

'*Are* you? Shit!'

I replaced the hairbrush on the crowded dressing-table, where you needed an A level in French to find your way around the little pots and perfume bottles.

'Do help yourself, Jaffa. They're all duty-free pongs. Not terribly romantic, is it? My old man, late for his plane, goes roaring like a bull into duty-free and grabs a bottle, any bottle, from the perfumery counter. "Got to keep the wife happy," he's thinking. "Take her a little prezzy." '

She looked sharply at my face.

'You're not wearing any slobby-dosh?'

'Pardon?'

'Meck-up, no meck-up?'

'No.'

'Shit! You mean that's just your face?'

'Yes.'

She ushered me out of the room and down the stairs. She laid her white hand on my arm.

'By the way, Jaffa, don't be offended, but never, never, say "pardon". "Pardon" is what belching business men say in bistros in Birmingham.'

Dodo joined us on the stairs. She was transformed, as I was. Her black hair was scraped back and twisted into a bun. Her dress was velvet and had no back to it. Her neck was clean. Caroline disapproved.

'Black again, Dodo?'

'Oh I couldn't wear a *colour*, Caroline. I'm not nearly happy enough.'

'It's time you got over Geoff now, Do. He's been mouldering in his coffin for three years.'

Dodo said to me, 'We'll go and see Geoff tomorrow. It is Sunday, isn't it . . . ? Yes, we'll take Geoff some flowers.'

'I'm meeting my brother's plane tomorrow,' I said.

'Time to do both.' Dodo squeezed my hand and we went into the dining-room.

Throughout dinner the company forced Dodo to tell amusing anecdotes about Cardboard City. Hardly anything she said was true. I didn't join in the laughter much. Cardboard City isn't funny. It's a real place.

The famous politician asked Dodo the question I'd been wanting to ask her myself, ever since we'd met.

'Why do I live in Cardboard City, instead of in this house? Well, let's see.'

She kept us waiting for her answer but eventually said: 'I *couldn't stand* to live in this house; Caroline wears rubber gloves when she wipes her bum, don't you, Caroline?'

'I fail to . . .' Caroline clamped her lips together.

Dodo went on. 'Anyway, I'm still officially loony; the police are looking for me.'

Nick said: 'She's compromising us *all* by her presence, especially you, Podger. If the press . . .'

Podger leaned forward over the table; one elbow made contact with a slice of Kiwi fruit left abandoned on a hexagonal plate, but nobody alerted him; he was too important.

'Why are you wanted by the police, Dodo?'

'Because I'm a murderer.'

The communal gasp almost put the candles out.

'I murdered Geoff.'

'Stop showing off, Dodo. Geoff's death was an accident, the coroner said. . . . God! Who'd have a sister like *her*?'

Nick appealed round the table but everyone was looking at Dodo, hoping for more revelations. Caroline drawled: 'That poxy cat killed Geoff. That cat lived so that Geoff might die.' Dodo sipped on her champagne and said, 'Yes, I really should have killed the cat. I made the wrong decision.'

After this, everyone, apart from me, relaxed. I was still tense from working out the cutlery. And the artichokes and the finger bowls. And the jokes. And the references. I felt suffocated by my awful,

awful proximity to the famous politician. I did hear some interesting talk, though. It was most enlightening. Scandal with a capital S. According to the table, all bishops and chief constables were buffoons; a member of the Royal Family was snorting cocaine; judges were 'senile old sods'; the Army, Airforce and Navy top brass were respectively 'gaga', 'psychopathic' and 'a snivelling sycophant'; and Podger's mistress was in Los Angeles having the fat sucked out of her thighs and knees, thus enabling her to wear the new short skirts.

Over coffee one of the guests, Amanda, said, 'Podgie, when are you and your mates going to be *sensible* about the unemployed?'

I breathed more easily.

'*You're spoiling* them, darling, doling out all this cash into their grimy little hands. It's no wonder they don't want to work. Who would?'

'Balls!' It was Dodo.

'I think *not* balls, Dodo.' Amanda was smiling. 'One only has to read the jobs columns in *The Times*. There's plenty of work for those who want it. Aren't I right, Podger?'

Podger lifted his famous face reluctantly. He didn't quite catch Amanda's eye, as he said: 'In the main you're right, of course, though . . .'

'You see, Dodo. The minister agrees with me.'

Caroline was lurching around the table taking photographs of her birthday guests with a polaroid camera. Podger pulled my head towards his and draped his hand casually over my bare shoulder. His index finger was a quarter of an inch from the swelling of my left breast. When the flash went off he opened his mouth, faking bonhomie; obviously he was used to having his photograph taken, and had developed good timing.

At twelve o'clock Caroline announced the end of her birthday, and the beginning of mine.

> Heppy birthday to you,
> Heppy birthday to you,
> Heppy birthday dear Jaffa,
> Heppy birthday tu-u-yew.

Dodo fell asleep with her head on the table, and everyone said, 'God is that the time? We *must* go.' But nobody did, they stayed on to talk.

AMANDA: You can say what you like about Hitler, but he knew a thing or two. He knew how to *prioritize*.

CAROLINE: Have you noticed, there's not a single yid around this table. Isn't it wonderful?

Laughter

PODGER: I say, we're being awfully Third Reich.

Loud laughter

ANNA [*journalist*]: I'm sick of seeing black faces in Harrods – either side of the counters.

Baying agreeing noises

DODO: I can't live in this house because I'm a communist. My dearest wish is that one day I shall see your grisly heads on the end of pikestaffs. Paraded . . . where shall we parade them, Jaffa?

ME: On Westminster Bridge.

Silence

Caroline said, 'OK Dodo, I thought you might amuse us for a few hours, but you're getting tiresome now. I'll order the car for you. Cardboard City, isn't it? You may have to direct the driver.'

We went upstairs to change our clothes, but Caroline followed and said to me: 'Keep the green frock, you stupid northern oik. Do you rally think *I'd* wear it after your nasty sweaty prole body has been in it?' Dodo grabbed Caroline's fingers and bent them back. Caroline screamed like a schoolgirl. Nick bounded up the stairs two at a time. He reached the two women and grappled them apart. His face was horribly contorted. 'Git owt of my harse, you detty little commie, and nivver, nivver come back!'

The dinner guests mobbed about on the landing, separating brother from sister, but not before Dodo had scratched Nick's face, and had drawn blood. Similar scenes can be seen and heard on the Grey Paths Estate any night of the week. The slight difference here was that the people screaming, fighting and bleeding had money, power and status – and knew they wouldn't be arrested for breaching the peace of Flood Street. Even though there was a policeman sitting in the kitchen.

We were burdened down with packages and suitcases as we left the house. Dodo had taken all of her clothes and some of Caroline's. We jammed everything into the boot of the big black car, then got in and settled down in the back seat. The car moved off.

113

'Driver, please put the interior light on. Jaffa, look what I nicked off the dining-room table.' Dodo showed me the polaroid photograph of myself – looking half naked – and the famous politician looking fully debauched, with his hand appearing to be holding firmly onto my left breast.

'Where are we going, madam?' asked the driver.

'The Ritz.'

'Thank you, madam.'

Dodo had stolen a thousand pounds from her brother's sock drawer. She justified this by saying that her brother was thoroughly corrupt, and that anyway half of the Flood Street house belonged to her; but Nick wouldn't sell until the Arabs started moving West. It all seemed quite fair to me.

The porters at the Ritz were very kind about the unwieldy luggage and within half an hour Dodo and I were exploring a suite of rooms. A laconic Italian waiter brought us champagne and hot buttered toast and told us that we were beautiful. Ten minutes later he was back with a basket of Norwegian wild flowers.

'Somebody die; shame to waste.'

In the bath I asked Dodo if she really was a communist. She got out of the foam and rummaged through her luggage and came back into the bathroom (*one* of the bathrooms) carrying a small card. She was a card-carrier all right.

There were four beds to choose from. We chose two and sank down to sleep. In the drowsy minutes before my eyes closed I told Dodo that my name was Coventry Dakin and that I had murdered Gerald Fox.

'I know,' said Dodo. 'Your face was plastered all over the papers last Saturday. True, *now* you don't look anything like your photograph in the papers, but I twigged. Clever, aren't I?'

In the morning Dodo felt guilty about staying at the Ritz so she overtipped the waiter who brought us our breakfast trolley and newspapers. I didn't feel a bit guilty; I loved everything. The thick bathrobes, the soap, the freshly squeezed orange juice, the warm croissants, the bacon, the gold furniture, the pink walls, the triple glazing, the hot water and the misty view across the park (Green Park, Dodo said).

Nick telephoned before we'd finished eating.

'You bloody little thief.'

'You bloody big thief.'

'I want my money back, and Caroline wants her Jean Muirs. I'll give you until midday and then I'm calling the police *and* the loony bin.'

We checked out of the Ritz at 11.55. We took a taxi to Cardboard City and stowed all the luggage inside our freezer-box house. James Spittlehouse was threatened into guarding our possessions.

'If you take your eyes off our house for one moment, Spittlehouse, we'll expose that virginal pink winkle of yours,' said Dodo.

Unfair, but effective. We left him eating the remains of our Ritz breakfast. He had a pink linen napkin tucked into the top of his greasy, buttoned-up overcoat. A croissant crumbled down his chest. He asked what time we'd be back. We said we didn't know.

We were busy women. We had things to do. Visit a grave and meet a plane.

29 Sunday Morning

Tennis Ball and Bread Knife looked across the breakfast table at each other. The BBC had just informed them that their daughter, Coventry, was in London, of all places.

'What's she doing in *London*?' said Coventry's father, as he rolled his little fat body away from the table.

Coventry's mother crinkled her lips together in cartoon style and said nothing. She disapproved of London. The popular press had informed her that London was entirely populated with dirty, drug-crazed pop stars and filthy communist councillors. True, the Queen lived there, but she was protected from the scum by a high wall and security patrols.

She cleared the breakfast table and then began the laborious task of washing up. Every bowl, plate, cup, saucer, knife, fork, spoon and eggcup was washed, rinsed three times and then polished with a sterilized tea towel before being put away into a daily disinfected cupboard.

Coventry's parents had not discussed the murder of Gerald Fox and their daughter's involvement in his death. They had told a baffled policewoman sent to interview them that they were 'clean people', who changed their bed sheets and towels *every day*, 'not weekly, like some dirty people'. When Coventry's mother was asked if her daughter had been having an affair with Gerald Fox, she had replied, 'I get through five bottles of disinfectant a week, don't I, father?'

Coventry's father had nodded and the policewoman had given up and left the antiseptic house.

As she placed the last apostle spoon in the crumbless drawer the front door bell rang and Bread Knife heard the voices of her grandchildren quarrelling in a desultory fashion on the doorstep. They always visited on Sunday morning. It was a great inconvenience.

'*Ask* before you borrow my things, Mary.'

'Oh shut your face, it's only a scarf.'

Before she opened the door, Bread Knife went to a cupboard and took out two plastic bags for her grandchildren's shoes. The children were in their stockinged feet by the time she had slipped the bolts and opened the mortice locks and removed the chains from the door.

''Lo, Nana. Mum's in London.'

Bread Knife noticed that John's fingernails were ragged and grimy. They produced a feeling of physical revulsion in her.

'We're going to look for her,' said Mary, placing her shoes in the plastic bag her grandmother was holding out.

'Well, young lady, you've been a bit lackadaisical with the Cherry Blossom, haven't you?' said Bread Knife, looking at Mary's scuffed black shoes through the plastic bag. The children padded through into the living-room and sat on the plastic-coated sofa. Tennis Ball bounced to his feet and greeted them. 'So she's in London.'

John said, 'Yeah, we're going down there.'

'*Up*,' said Mary, 'It's *up* to London.'

'Down,' said John.

'Up,' said Mary.

'Don't roarm about like that,' said their little fat tennis ball of a granddad. 'You're wrinkling the plastic covers.'

Through the kitchen doorway their grandmother could be seen furiously cleaning their sinful shoes.

30 Sly Closes In

During the time it took Sidney's erection to subside, Inspector Sly did ridiculous, futile pressing up and down actions on the knobs of the telephone receiver. After twenty seconds of this, he conceded that Sidney had put the phone down at the other end. Sly replaced his own handset and commanded a young dogsbody in uniform to order a car and a driver. He was 'going to the Smoke', he said.

He rang Derek at home. Did Derek know if his wife had friends or relations in London? Derek spoke (and thought) of London as being as far away and remote as Saturn. No, they had never been to *London*. They knew no Londoners.

Inspector Sly said he was travelling down tomorrow, 'weather permitting'.

He made it sound as though his transportation was to be a team of huskies, pulling a provision-laden sledge. He intimated that the journey would be fraught with dangers, that the elements of air, earth, water and fire would be ranged against him. In a sense he was right. The M1 motorway demanded – and got – human sacrifices every day of the week.

Sly then rang his wife and ordered her to pack a small suitcase. He was 'closing in on Coventry Dakin', and 'might be gone for some time'. Sly's wife made jubilant, arm-stabbing-the-air gestures at the news of his absence; but was careful to keep her voice under control. Such duplicity was second nature to her now.

She had married Sly twenty-seven years ago, when he had been a police cadet with ideals and she had been a typist with a salary. She'd seen her husband change into a barbarian. It was all those criminals he mixed with, she thought. Mrs Sly went into the utility room and started to iron her husband's vast cotton shirts.

Detective Inspector Sly started to prepare for the next day. He packed his brief-case with files, floppy discs and fistfuls of photographs in which Coventry could be seen dancing, swimming and digging; with new-born babies; twirling a hula hoop around her waist; sitting on a rug in a park, blinking into the sun; peeling potatoes; changing a nappy; reading the *Daily Mirror* on a park bench. There was Coventry with Mary, with John; Coventry in trousers, shorts, overcoats, summer frocks; and finally Coventry pointing a gun at the camera, the photograph that Sly had picked out to be used by what he called the 'meeja'.

31 I Leave the City

'Geoffrey's over there.'

Dodo pointed to a distant copse of trees. We were in the country; standing in a graveyard. A dark church glowered over us. Lichened gravestones lurched at crazy angles. We walked through long, wet grass to Geoff's grave. He was lying under a pink and grey marble slab; his was a designer grave.

A tombstone said:

> Geoff is here, he was Dodo's husband.
> She loved him.
> Born 1946, died 1985.

A Coca Cola bottle stood next to the tombstone. Beetles swam about in the inch or so of water in the bottom.

I said, 'A *Coca Cola bottle*?'

Dodo replied, 'The villagers nick the vases. Geoff wouldn't have minded; he had a tremendous sense of humour.'

She had brought a small bunch of freesias and now she stuck them into the bottle and fiddled with them until she was satisfied, then she placed the bottle in the dead centre of the slab and walked away. I caught up with her by the dank yew hedge which lined the path to the churchyard gate. She smiled and said, 'Right, that's the husband's grave visited, now to meet the brother's plane.'

The London cab we had come in was waiting for us outside in the narrow lane. The driver was looking around suspiciously at the trees and fields. He looked as though he was in the first stages of an agoraphobic panic attack. We had lured him into the countryside by showing him many twenty-pound notes. He only brightened up when Dodo said, 'Gatwick Airport, please.'

But before the taxi could draw away a herd of cattle turned the corner of the lane and trotted up to the taxi on their spindly legs. We were soon surrounded by cows who gazed curiously into the cab with their lovely eyes.

'Who's in charge of 'em?' shouted the cab driver to himself.

'Cows are so *camp*,' said Dodo. 'Such OTT eyelashes. They always remind me of Danny La Rue.'

'I hope he keeps his arse cleaner than *them*,' said the driver, looking with disgust at the casually excreting animals.

A row of low terraced cottages stood opposite the church. Out of a rustic door came a woman carrying a shallow wicker basket. She stood in the tiny garden watching the cows and then stooped down to pick nasturtium flowers, which she laid in her basket. She looked so simple and charming in her pretty full-skirted dress, her hair tied back with a ribbon. Even the green wellingtons she wore didn't seem inappropriate. I remarked on her to Dodo.

'Oh *her*,' said Dodo. 'That's Veronica Minton. She's a merchant banker. She's got a telex in her back parlour.' Dodo wound down her window and shouted: 'Veronica!'

Veronica turned around and saw Dodo. She didn't look too pleased, but she came over to the taxi.

'Dodo,' she said. 'Been to Geoff's grave?'

'Yes. How's the country?'

'Bloody.'

'Bloody?'

'Yes, we're selling up.'

'Why?'

'The noise and inconvenience and the *vandalism*. You wouldn't believe it. Have you seen what the village yobs have written on the War Memorial? And these sodding *cows*. Four times a day they pass our cottage. The *shit* and the *smell* and the tractor fumes. And the noise when the village pub chucks out. And, there's nowhere for the kids to play. And we've been burgled three times and nothing will *grow*.'

'Your nasturtiums look pretty,' said Dodo.

'Yes,' said Veronica bitterly. 'They thrive in poor soil.'

'Where will you be moving to?' asked Dodo.

'Somewhere quiet,' said Veronica, 'in Clapham.'

A twelve-year-old-looking boy came round the bend in the lane. He was swishing a cane towards a few recalcitrant cows. The taxi driver started his engine and began to creep through the gaps between the animals. The boy shrieked, 'You mad bugger, watch them cows!' The driver shook his fist out of the window in classic fashion and shouted, 'Get them bleedin' scumbags out of my way, sonny, before I mow the bleeders down.'

Veronica sighed deeply and said, 'See? The countryside is so *unpleasant*; it brings out the worst in people.'

As we careered through the village I noticed that the village shop was called a 'Provision Centre' and that the War Memorial was covered in graffiti, 'Veronica sucks' being the most prominent. Large prairie-like fields stretched into the far distance. Dodo was quiet, only stirring herself to point out a large house just visible through wooded grounds.

'Geoff was born there.'

I asked, 'Do his family still live there?'

'No, it's a retirement home for gentlefolk now.'

'A long walk to the Provision Centre,' I said.

Dodo laughed and was silent.

I had never been on a plane, or visited an airport. Gatwick looked like a rat's maze to me, but Dodo seemed to know exactly where to go and which computerized sign to read. She told me that Sidney's plane was due to land at 6.10 p.m.

We had three hours and five minutes to kill, so we had a meal in the restaurant. We sat by the window so that Dodo could watch the planes taking off and landing. It looked a risky business.

Four American men came and sat at the next table to us. They ordered steaks in loud, happy voices. They called the old waitress 'ma'am' and asked for her advice on their choice of side salads. When she'd hobbled off with their large order, they lit cigarettes and began to talk business. A man in an orange and green checked jacket resumed a previous conversation.

'Sure, singing telegrams are kinda old news. I mean, you *know* you're gonna get one on your birthday, yeah?'

The other three Americans said: 'Yeah.'

'And other *happy* occasions. Yeah?'

'Yeah.'

'So the market's saturated with two-bit outfits all over Europe, and they got King Kong-o-grams, Roly-Poly grams, Kisso-grams . . .'

Another man with a mad haircut cut in: 'Sure, we know, Wayne. Jeez, he's here in England one week and the guy is so *slow* already.'

Wayne laughed with the others. 'Yeah, I guess I caught it from the British Railroad Company.'

Laugh? They couldn't stop. Eventually Wayne was able to go on. After wiping his eyes he said, 'So the market's static, there's no innovation . . . agree?'

'Sure for Chrissake, Wayne . . . !'

'Hey don't push me, Conroy. I gotta *explain*. I'm gonna spring a new concept on ya. You ready?'

'So, *spring*.'

'Singing telegrams for *unhappy* occasions.'

'Unhappy?'

'Yeah, divorce, bereavement, splitting, telling a chick she's too fat or some'pn' . . . hey, Steel, what's the worst thing you'd ever have to tell your mother?'

'That I'm Aids positive?'

'No, we're talking hypothesis here. This bad news is to do with *her*. She's old, she's ill . . .'

'She's dying?'

'Yeah. *You* don't wanna tell her, do you, Steel? . . . She's terminal.'

'No *sir*.'

'The doctor don't wanna do it . . .'

'Uh-huh.'

'So you ring and order a terminal-a-gram.'

'A what?'

'A terminal-a-gram.'

Wayne stood by Steel's chair; he started to sing to the tune 'Whistle While You Work':

> Oh happy, happy day!
> You're going to pass away . . .

Steel burst out, 'Wayne, that is grossly *gross*.'

Conroy said, 'Cool it, Steel. This could *be*. Got something for announcing a divorce to your wife?'

Wayne thought for a moment and stood again and sang to the tune of 'Some Enchanted Evening':

> Your husband doesn't love you:
> He's been to see a lawyer.
>
> The hearing's in November
> Inside a crowded room . . .

The fourth man burst out: 'It's phenomenal. Think of it! Driving examiners don't have to worry about failing candidates; they have regular depot-based bad-news-o'-persons to do it for them.' He sang to 'The Lady Is a Tramp':

> You took that corner so dangerously fast,
> You passed a red light,
> So, gal, you ain't
> Passed.

Wayne whooped and slapped the fourth man on the shoulders and said, 'Burdock, you're *beautiful*. I know it's gonna *work*. Fifty thousand dollars each and we can do it. Open the first office in London, the time's right.'

Their meal arrived and Steel and Conroy and Wayne and Burdock fell onto the tiny English steaks with grunts and blunt knives.

'Hey, ma'am,' shouted Wayne to the waitress. 'You gotta bottle of good French wine there? We gotta celebration here.'

The waitress brought a bottle of Niersteiner which, Dodo whispered, was German, but the Americans didn't know or didn't notice. They were happily engaged in singing little ditties about life's more unpleasant aspects:

> Yesterday, all your troubles seemed so far away,
> Now the cops have towed your car away! . . .

32 The Good Policeman Horsefield

Sly had ordered the police driver to pull over onto the hard shoulder of the motorway. They were just outside Newport Pagnell. He confronted the young policeman as they swopped places round the bonnet of the car.

'What are you, a nancy boy? What's with this ninety miles an hour pussyfooting around crap? I'm in a hurry, boy. This is a *murder* investigation.'

'There's a lot of traffic on the road, sir,' the young man said, looking at the lorries hurtling by in unbroken convoys.

'I'll show you how to manage bleedin' *traffic*,' snarled Sly. 'Get in the passenger seat.'

In the back seat of the police car sat Detective Sergeant Horsefield. He had known this was going to happen. Something like it always did. But he feared Inspector Sly more than he feared death on the motorway, so he whispered a prayer to Our Lady under his breath and braced his feet on the floor and closed his eyes. Sly pulled straight out in front of a juggernaut, causing it to make an emergency stop. Then he overtook (on the inside) a minibus full of brass band players and swerved violently into the fast lane, where he stayed by means of the police siren and by forcing the cars ahead to move out of his way. At times the speedometer touched a hundred and twenty miles an hour.

Inside the car nobody spoke. Horsefield wished now that he had made his will, as his wife had often suggested. Horsefield was a nice man. He believed in the law and justice, but not necessarily in that order. He had a degree and an educated accent and, despite these handicaps, had made friends and even influenced people in the police force. Horsefield was secretly and devoutly religious. He said his prayers in the bathroom at night, kneeling on the bath mat and folding his hands together like a child.

33 About to Land

Sidney Lambert was never happier than when he was on an aeroplane: nobody could get to him. He had food, drink; his beloved wife was sitting in the next seat; and, best of all, throughout the flight there was the titillating threat of sudden death, which always added a tang to life. Sidney leaned back in his seat, squashing the person behind him. He and Ruth were wearing all white, essential for showing off the tan to the October pasty faces back in England.

Above his head, stowed away in the baggage cupboards, were the crudely painted souvenir plates and bottles of *vinho verde* he'd bought in the duty-free at Faro Airport. Ruth was wearing a new gold and diamond ring, a present for being a good girl, which cost well above the allowance permitted by poxy English Customs. So that was all right. He was happy, Ruth was happy and the rest of the world could go and screw itself.

To tell the truth he wouldn't actually mind dying *now* – if he had to die – was forced to by God. Yes, he'd choose *now*. Fold Ruth into his arms and go down in the water, or up in the flames together. There'd be time for a last drink, wouldn't there? And if Ruth started screaming, he'd knock her out. He didn't need Ruth to be conscious, she just had to be *there*.

Shame about poor old Cov. What a poxy mess she'd got herself into! Still, it wasn't his mess. He'd do his best to help her, of course he would, but only up to a point. Be fair. He and Ruth had their own lives to lead, and nothing was going to get in the way of that. No way. If the police were at the airport it wouldn't bother him that much, not really. He'd talk his way out. Wouldn't he? Christ. Bloody *baby* started *crying*. He'd give it two minutes, no, *one* minute and then he'd ring for the stewardess and complain. If there was one thing he couldn't *tolerate, stand*, it was a bloody baby crying. Good job Ruth had been sensible, listened to reason about those abortions. Would they have had foreign holidays, villas and private swimming pools if they had *babies* to cart round, plus all the gubbins babies need? No. Course not. And would their house be the immaculate white-carpeted little palace it was with toddlers breaking the joint up? No way. Look how kids had ruined their wedding day, shouting out in church and fartarsing about during the reception. He'd *told* Ruth's mother to put 'strictly no children' on the invitations, but the stupid cow-faced bag had said it would 'offend the mutual families'. He was glad that Ruth had seen the light about her mother.

'Right, kid, you've got five seconds of screaming left before your Uncle Sidney presses his buzzer. I mean for Jesus Christ on earth's sake, the little moon-headed bleeder's travelling *free*. I've paid eighty-nine pounds return, twice.'

Ruth tried to divert Sidney from the horrible noise. 'Poor little kiddie,' she thought, 'I'd soon stop it crying, bless it.'

'Sidney, how long before we get to Gatwick?'

'An hour.'

'Lovely. Thank you, Sidney.'

In a cafeteria at Gatwick Airport Detective Sergeant Horsefield watched Detective Inspector Sly shovel eggs, bacon, fried bread, mushrooms, baked beans, chips and bread and butter into his rapacious mouth.

'I've seen wild boars with better manners,' thought Horsefield. He picked at his own, more austere, food and didn't look up again until he'd eaten every leaf, pulse and grain. Then he placed his knife and fork on the empty plate, as though they were religious artefacts. Sly pulled a banana split towards him and plunged a spoon into the baroque squirts of cream with which it was decorated. He spoke: 'Ri–, 'ets ge– 'orted.'

'Sorry?'

Sly swallowed four hundred and fifty calories and said: 'I *said*, let's get sorted. His plane lands in forty-five minutes, right? So when we've had our coffee we'll liaise with the uniformed plods and airport security and sort out who's doing what, right? Are you listening, Horsefield? I said *right*.'

'Yes, I heard you, sir.'

'When I say *right*, I'm asking you a *question*; and a question needs an answer, right?'

'Oh, right, sir, right.'

'Right. What I'd *like* to do is arrest him on the plane.'

'Oh?'

'Saw it done on a film once. Very effective. Spy it was, trying to defecate to the East.'

Horsefield laughed. He was pleased and also relieved at this proof that Sly had a sense of humour. However, Sly was not laughing.

'What's so funny?'

'To *defecate* to the East, sir.'

'I'm not with you, Horsefield. Defecating to the East is a serious matter. Right?'

'Right!'

Horsefield's body imploded with suppressed laughter. Every orifice had to be slammed shut. Tight. Keep it *in*, Horsefield. To laugh now could cost you promotion, early retirement and a good pension.

'So, Horsefield, I *will* go on the plane and you can wait at Arrivals in case that murdering bitch is daft enough to turn up with a bunch of daffs and a welcome home kiss. Be back in a bit. Percy needs pointing.'

Sly lumbered his way through the fragile café furniture towards the lavatory sign. Horsefield laughed and laughed and laughed. The laughing policeman and no need to put a penny in the slot, either. When he'd recovered himself Horsefield went to a telephone and phoned home. His small son answered the phone.

'This is Matthew John James Horsefield speakin' on the phone at the moment. Which person do you want to have a talk to?'

Horsefield laughed again at the thoroughness of the three-year-old's telephone manner.

'It's Daddy.'

''Lo Dad, it's Matthew John James Horsefield talkin'.'

'Yes, I know; you said. Is Mummy there?'

'No, she's in the kitchen; there's only me here.'

'Can you go and fetch Mummy?'

'Yes.'

Horsefield heard the receiver drop abruptly then heard it cracking against the wall as it swung loose on its cord. How many times had he told that kid not to . . . ?

'Darling?'

'Darling, I just rang to tell you . . .'

'Nothing wrong?'

'No, Sly drove down, though!'

'Oh, poor you.'

'What are you cooking?'

'Green mashed potatoes and blue fish fingers.'

'Oh.'

His little son had watched a cookery item on children's television. Horsefield had gone out in his lunch break in the week and bought six bottles of food colouring. His wife had told him off and accused him of spoiling the boy.

'I'll have to go, Malcolm.' Horsefield was touched, she rarely used his Christian name. 'The stove's on and . . .'

'Let me say goodbye to Matthew.'

He heard his son's feet clumping across the parquet of the hall floor. He guessed that he was still wearing his new winter boots, bought earlier that day.

''Bye Matthew, see you tomorrow.'

'Why?'

'Because I'm far away, in London.'

'Why?'

'Because I'm at work.'

'Why?'

'To get money to buy you new boots. That's *it*. Matthew, don't ask any more questions.'

'Why?'

'Because it drives me mad, you know it does. I'm going now. Tell Mummy I love her.'

'Tell Mummy I love her,' Matthew repeated.

'No, tell Mummy *I* love her. Not you.'

His wife came back on the phone. 'You've made him cry! What did you say?'

'I only raised my voice!'

'Malcolm!'

'Oh Barbara, what am I doing here? I want to be there, at home.' Sly was making manic faces through the plastic hood of the telephone booth. Horsefield whispered, '*I love you*,' and put the phone down.

Mrs Horsefield was astonished at the urgency in her husband's voice. She looked forward very much indeed to his homecoming.

34 Transition

It didn't take long for me to become wildly excited by Gatwick Airport. It was the most romantic place I'd ever visited. At the end of the tunnels and walkways were jungles and deserts and ancient cities; there were possibilities. I asked Dodo how I could get a passport.

'It would be difficult, but not impossibly so. Why, darling? Where do you want to go?'

'Anywhere,' I said. I wanted to leave the ground and pierce the sky, and disappear inside the clouds.

I'm forty and I've never flown in an aeroplane; never driven a car; never, as an adult, been to the theatre or been ice-skating; never played tennis or been to a night-club; never eaten Chinese food in a Chinese restaurant, worn pretty underwear or had a bank account or talked about sex, money and politics in mixed company. What *is* the Dow Jones Index. I admit, I don't know. I'm an ignorant woman. How has this happened? When I was little I was considered clever; I won certificates for cycling proficiency, swimming and hurdling. And the books I used to read when I was sixteen! Adult books about important issues. Why did I stop reading the books?

It's not Derek's fault, it's really not. It's not Derek's fault. And I'm not going to blame John and Mary either; it's my own fault. I became timid and quiet and frightened of imposing myself. Something has happened to me. Killing Gerald Fox has broken the spell. I'm ready to fly. I know this is hard on Gerald Fox.

Only one more plane is due from the Algarve this evening. Our plan is to stand back and wait for Sidney and Ruth to come through into the Arrivals lounge. We will then follow them at a distance. We will be heavily disguised and when we consider it safe, I will make myself known. I don't know what will happen then. I want to ask Sidney to look after my children until I can send for them and look after them myself. Again, I don't know how Sidney will react. He pretends not to like children but I'm sure he must have a soft spot for *my* kids. They are so nice, I don't see how anybody could dislike them. It is now over a week since I saw them and in that time not an hour has gone by that I haven't thought about them. They are splinters in my brain. I will take them with me everywhere I go for the rest of my life. Only my own death will release me from them.

I haven't missed Derek. But I feel very sad about leaving him to cope on his own and I hope he'll find somebody to love him one day. A good listener, who likes tortoises and can do the foxtrot, would be ideal.

Dodo has been on the telephone to her brother for over twenty minutes. I don't know what she's saying; all I know is that she looks serious and insistent and she is doing most of the talking. I wish she would hurry; Sidney's plane is due to land in thirty-five minutes.

35 Podger's World Collapses

Podger was in the bath reading the *News of the World* when Nicholas Cutbush rang. His wife answered the phone and at first refused to put the call through to their *en suite* bathroom. 'Honestly Nick, it's the only time he gets to truly relax all week, I'm furious with you.'

Nicholas sounded hysterical as he said, 'Unless I speak to him *now* he'll be out on his arse and reading the Sits Vac by Tuesday morning.' So she put him through and scrambled the phone, as she had scrambled the eggs earlier in the day.

'Nick, what is it?'

'My bloody sister's got a photograph of you fondling the left breast of a fugitive murderess.'

'Which fugitive murderess?'

'For fuck's sake, Podger, how many do you know? *Jaffa!* The dinner party. Caroline took your pic. . .'

'Oh *Jaffa*. *She* did a murder? Christ!'

'Christ indeed. Jaffa is Coventry Dakin.'

'Who?'

'Coventry Dakin, she smashed a bloke's head in with a doll. It's been on the front page of every . . .'

'Nick, I'm finished.'

'You're not, not yet. Dodo wants two false passports.'

'Right.'

'And, of course, money.'

'Of course.'

'Today.'

'But it's Sunday afternoon.'

'If she doesn't get them today she sends the photo round to Paul Foot in a minicab.'

'Mike's nephew?'

'Well it wouldn't be Paul Foot, chiropodist, would it? Or Paul Foot, interior decorator? Yes, Paul Foot, *investigative journalist*, committed socialist.'

'Oh God! Oh God! . . . Nick, this is in confidence. Herself the PM is announcing the date of the by-elections tomorrow.'

'Oh lovely, marvellous, perfect timing.'

'Nick, shouldn't I just resign?'

'You've only been doing the job a bloody month, if that.'

'But Profumo, Thorpe, Parkinson, Archer . . . We'll never get away with . . .'

'You utter, utter prat, Podger. If we lose those by-elections the money will flood out of the country and leave us up shit street.'

'It was your wife who took my photograph. It's all your fault. One assumes when one goes to dinner that one's amongst friends or, at the very least, vetted strangers.'

'OK, OK. Sorry Podge. Now calm down, calm down. Phone the Duty Officer and arrange the passports. You know Dodo and Jaffa: both forty-ish, no distinguishing marks, one dark, one redhead, both about five foot seven . . . they're having their passport photos taken now.'

'All right. Can I finish my bath now?'

'There's something else, Podger.'

'Go on.'

'You'll say it's impossible, but it *has to be done*.'

As Podger listened the bath water cooled around his belly and the scum rose to the surface.

36 I Face Myself

Dodo came off the phone and said: 'Let's have our photograph taken in one of those dinky little booths.'

I chose the blue background curtain, adjusted the winding stool and sat down and composed myself in front of the mirror. I wanted to appear serious, clever, happy, sad, sexy, detached, mysterious and kind; but when the sticky photographs spewed out of the machine I was disappointed.

'What do you think?' I asked Dodo, when she came back from wherever she'd been with a set of stationery and stamps.

'You look pale, startled, and thoroughly forty,' she said, putting the stamps on the envelopes. Dodo doesn't mince her words, she grinds them into paste. 'What you need, Jaffa dear, is a holiday.'

Dodo went into the booth and stayed in there until eight photographs had been taken. The first four were of Dodo, looking stern. The second four were of Dodo laughing and holding up the photograph of me and Podger.

'Just for the record,' she said, as she waved the second strip around in the air to dry.

'What are you going to do with those?' I asked.

'Escape,' she said. 'And take you with me, if you want to come.'

'Where are we escaping to?' I asked.

'Anywhere in the world,' she said. 'Perhaps the Welsh mountains.'

At the time I thought she was joking, or perhaps fantasizing. She took my photographs from me and put them inside her big leather shoulder-bag, saying, 'They'll be safer in here.'

I thought it a strange thing to do because Dodo knows that I am very careful with my possessions. I've never lost anything I didn't want to lose. I've had the same front door key for nineteen years, whereas my precious daughter Mary has lost ten keys in four years. Oh my sweet, lovely Mary, I'm pining for you. How surprised you'd be to read these words. We were not an openly affectionate family. We stopped touching each other and swopping endearments long ago, and became embarrassed and awkward in each other's company.

I'm so sorry this happened. Dearest Mary, I want you to stay on at school and have an education; it's the only dignified way out of Grey Paths Council Estate. We are not lost to each other, Mary. We are bound by a cord far stronger than the umbilical one that was cut and tied on the day you were born to me. Dear Mary, don't stoop and slouch, walk proudly with your shoulders back. And look around, don't look away. And speak out clearly, don't mumble. Don't lie or dissemble, or only tell people what you think will please them. And don't forget me, Mary. Remember that I loved you. Oh, and try very hard not to lose your front door key. And always, always, be kind.

Sidney's plane has landed! Dodo, who knows about these things, says that it takes at least twenty minutes to get through Passport Control, Baggage Reclaim and Customs. So, to kill more time we spend more of the stolen money and buy sweaters, gloves, scarves, and woolly hats. Dodo says that we will need warm clothes, but won't say why. I think we are escaping to the Welsh mountains after seeing Sidney. I hope so. Though I will look silly, not to mention conspicuous, climbing mountains in my leopard-skin coat.

My darling son went to Wales for a weekend when he was fourteen. The school organized it, but it was a business called 'Mobile Adventure' that actually took him and eight other children. They left our gently undulating county in a minibus and drove to wild Wales and walked a mountain ridge. My son still had his head in the clouds when he arrived home. I was pleased that he had seen other horizons. A young woman called Andrea had been responsible for him abseiling down a rock face.

Dear John, I hope that you will never forget that you once put your life in such safe, womanly hands.

37 Bradford Treads the Grey Paths

Bradford Keynes stood outside Number 13 Badger's Copse Close, Grey Paths Estate. He now knew that Lauren McSkye was also Coventry Dakin and he loved her more than ever. He could hardly believe that such a gorgeous woman had spent the majority of her adult years in such an abysmal place, had been obliged to tread these rancid grey pavements and look out upon such a lustreless landscape. He was not surprised that such a passionate, full-blooded woman had resorted to murder. She was an enchantress and needed to live in a magical place, not this pettifogging collection of concrete and brick they called an estate. His artist's eye was repelled by the T-squared design of the houses, with their skimpy front doors and meagre garden paths. He thought: 'This is nothingness' and he thanked a God he didn't believe in for his own quirky inner city terrace with its corner shop and Lowry matchsticks walking by his front room window. He scorned the nonsensical pseudo-Georgian front door and windows of Lauren's house.

'She's married to a parvenu,' he thought and, fired by curiosity, he walked up the path and rang the bell.

'If I Ruled the World' chimed inside the house and Derek Dakin opened the door as far as the security chain would allow. Bradford had not expected anybody so *old*. This guy must be forty-five at least. He had prepared nothing to say.

'Mr Dakin?'

'Yes?'

'I'm a friend of your wife's.'

'*I* don't know you.'

'No. I did *say* I was a friend of your *wife's*.'

'But I know *both* of my wife's friends. Are you sure you've got the right address?'

'Your wife is a very talented artist.'

'Yes, you've got the wrong house, young man. Now, if you wouldn't mind . . .'

'Could you give me something of hers? I'd like a keepsake, a token, something I can hold . . .'

Bradford's bushy beard was poking through the chain length of the open door. He hadn't meant to sound so subservient, but he couldn't pull himself together at all. Oh the humiliation! He knew he would hate himself tomorrow. He'd read about love and how it reduced people to staging histrionic scenes but he couldn't believe he was taking part in one himself. He'd learned, from reading Jung, that he was an introvert.

'A handkerchief would do. Is there anything in the washing?'

'No, go away. Take your foot and your beard out of my hallway.'

'I love her, I love your wife and when I find her I'm going to take her away and keep her to myself!' Bradford hadn't known he was capable of shouting with such passion.

'You'll wait for her to come out of prison, will you?' said Derek.

'Why? Is she *in* prison?'

'No,' said Derek. 'But when she's captured she will be.'

'Then I'll pitch a tent outside the prison gates.'

'The authorities would never allow it. You'd be contravening several by-laws.'

'I'll hire a plane to fly over the prison. It will carry a banner: I LOVE YOU LAUREN McSKYE. She'd look out of her little barred window and see it.'

'Lauren McSkye?' said Derek with relief. 'I *said* you'd got the wrong address. My wife's name is Dakin, Mrs Derek Dakin.'

Derek kicked Bradford's foot out onto the doorstep and slammed the door, trapping the end of the madman's straggling beard. Bradford screamed in pain but Derek did not dare risk opening the door and confronting the maniac again, so he hurried to the kitchen, found the scissors and passed them out through the letter-box to Bradford who was forced to trim his beard by four inches. Bradford posted the ginger hairs back through the letter-box but Derek didn't want to be accused of theft, so he posted them back to Bradford. He had enough on his plate: the children had been told to be home by two-thirty, but there was no sign of them and it was now four-fifteen and their Sunday dinners were dehydrating in the oven.

Derek turned the gas down and went outside to his shed. He had his tortoises to prepare for hibernation. 'Lucky little things,' said Derek, stroking the waving prehistoric heads. 'You're well out of it.'

38 The Young Dakins Grow Up

The young Dakins got off the coach at Gatwick and hurried into the Arrivals hall. They had quarrelled throughout the journey. It was Mary's idea to meet Uncle Sid and Aunty Ruth off the plane. 'We'll ask Uncle Sid to drive us round London, perhaps we'll see Mum.'

'Mary, do you know what the population of London *is*? We're talking in *millions*.'

'It's worth a try though, isn't it?'

'S'pose so, but don't get your hopes up. She's not such a dibbo as to be standing about in Trafalgar Square or anywhere famous, is she?'

'I can't imagine Mum in *London*, can you, John? You know – walking about and sleeping somewhere different from home. She's too shy and quiet.'

'She's not all *that* shy,' said John with heavy-hinting emphasis. He was thinking about his mother's secret diary, which he was carrying about in the inside pocket of his bomber jacket.

'She *is* shy. What about that time she won at bingo but she daren't shout out?'

John said, 'She'd been brought up not to shout in public. It wasn't her fault, was it?'

'But she sat there and let thirty-five pounds be added to the accumulator! All she had to do was shout "House!".'

'There's more to Mum than you think,' said John. 'There's more to her than meets the eye.'

'You don't think her and Gerald Fox were in love, do you?'

'I *know* they weren't.'

'How would *you* know?' Mary was infuriated by John's smugness.

John said: 'Look, I'm not in the mood for arguing now or ever again, so let's just *not* argue, eh?'

'What, never?'

'Yeah, I'm sick of it; it does my head in.'

'But what if I'm right and you're wrong, or you're right and I'm . . .?'

138

'Then just *say* something and I'll do the same, agree? But let's not *argue*. And . . .'

'Yeah?'

'You've got your gold chain in your mouth again. It drives me mad. Sorry, but it does.'

'Oh! John?'

'Yeah?'

'I'm not doing your washing any more, or your ironing. Sorry, but I'm not.'

'Fair enough.'

They were each amazed at how calmly the other took these remarks, and for the first time in their lives they almost liked each other and, for no reason they could explain at the time, they felt what it must be like to be grown-up.

They took their places on the periphery of the crowds waiting at the Arrivals barrier, and watched for Uncle Sid and Aunty Ruth to emerge from the Customs Hall. They both hoped that Sid was in a good mood and would be amenable to driving around London. You never knew with Sid; he was a very perplexing person.

39 Beautiful Children

There had been continual announcements on the airport public address system, and although I'd heard them I hadn't listened to what they were saying. But now my ears strained to catch every word.

'Will John Dakin please go to the Information Desk. John Dakin to the Information Desk.'

'That's my son's name,' I said to Dodo.

'There must be *thousands* of John Dakins,' she replied, but she looked apprehensive.

'Where is the Information Desk? *Where is it, Dodo?*'

'I'll show you, but please, Jaffa, keep your distance; and don't do anything silly, promise, darling?'

We left the cafeteria and looked over the balcony. The Information Desk was directly below us. My daughter Mary was standing at the desk looking worried. She was wearing her best coat and her fair hair was arranged in a new spiky style and appeared to be covered in a sticky substance.

I said, 'What has she got on her pretty hair?'

'Gel,' said Dodo; then, 'She's astonishingly like the old you, isn't she?'

As we watched, my golden-haired son walked through the crowd and tapped Mary on the shoulder. She turned round and they smiled at each other. They looked relieved.

'If you go to them now you'll end up in prison and you'll break their hearts. Don't go, Jaffa!'

I couldn't take my eyes off my beautiful children.

'Dodo, quickly, go and tell them I'm here . . . please, Dodo.'

Dodo walked slowly down the stairs and joined my children. It was a bizarre sight, one I had never expected to see; these people belonged in different compartments. Now Dodo was *talking* to them. They were looking around. They saw me. Dodo spoke sharply to them and they looked away at once. I strained towards my children. I wanted them so strongly that I felt weak and light-headed and had to stop myself making silly whimpering noises of desire.

John and Mary walked away, stiff and self-conscious; and Dodo rejoined me and said, 'They are going to get into a black cab. It will drive around the airport perimeter once and then return to the cab rank and pick you up. Here's your cab fare.' She gave me a twenty-pound note. She looked sick with fear.

She said, 'I never had a child, apart from Geoff. Now that he's dead, I wish I had; though you're never free again, are you? Am I right?'

I said that yes, she was right. Once you've had a child you're never free.

Dodo asked if I was still interested in escaping. I said I didn't know. A silence fell between us. Eventually I asked Dodo why the announcement had gone out asking John to report to the desk. 'They lost each other in the crowd, then wandered around looking for each other. They're here to meet Sidney – like you.'

40 Inspector Sly Gets His Man

Sidney had been at the buzzer again.

The stewardess hurried down the aisle and bent her Max Factored face over Sidney.

'We're delayed because of a technical fault, sir,' she lied. 'Please keep in your seat.'

'But we've been on the ground for over an hour. What sort of technical fault?'

'They know what they're doing, Sid,' said Ruth. This mild rebuke from Ruth surprised Sidney; it also frightened him. He remembered that Ruth had refused to have sex with him yesterday and that she had answered the telephone against his wishes. True, there had been no more evidence of Ruth's insurgency – until now.

'They obviously *don't* know what they're doing, Ruth; somebody has cocked something up. I'm getting off this plane, now!'

'Please sir, we've got our orders to let nobody off the plane.' Sweat bubbled through the stewardess's pancake foundation. A tendril of hair escaped from her chignon. She now looked human, like a real person, instead of a public relations cipher. A large, bulky man made his way, sideways on, down the narrow aisle. Inspector Sly was about to get his man. The stewardess pointed at Sidney, then stood aside to enable the law to take its course.

'Sidney Lambert? I'm Detective Inspector Sly. Come with me please, and don't ask why, or where or what for. I'm a busy man so let's skip the details. Stand up now and come with me.'

Sidney said, 'Why? Where? What for?'

Ruth said: 'They know about the ring, Sid!' Ruth took off her new gold and diamond ring and gave it to Inspector Sly, who turned it over in his hands, said, 'Very nice' and, to her surprise, gave it back.

'It's to do with Coventry then, is it?' said Sidney, as he and Sly and several extraneous policemen tramped down the aluminium steps from the aeroplane.

'Yes,' said Sly. 'I'm going to keep you in custody and squeeze your head now and again until you tell me where she's hiding. I've got a short break due to me next week, bird-watching in Norfolk, and I want this case wrapped up and nice and tidy before I pack my binoculars.'

Sidney shivered in his thin white clothes. After Portugal, England looked dull and washed out; the lousy weather was in one of its in-between moods: a bit cold, a bit wet, a bit misty, a bit depressing all round. As they walked across the tarmac Sidney looked at the shut-in English faces around him. 'They're all sexually repressed in England,' thought Sidney, temporarily distancing himself from his compatriots.

'What will happen to my wife?' he asked Sly.

'Dunno and don't care, Sid, my boy. She'll either go home to the Midlands or hang about here waiting for you, won't she?'

'All I can tell you is that Coventry is in London,' said Sidney.

Sly asked: 'Would that be Greater London, Mr Lambert, or the City of London? Perhaps you'd like to give me her address now? You needn't bother with the postcode.'

When they got inside the airport terminal, Sidney searched for his cigarettes, then cursed the vanity that had resulted in him buying skin-tight trousers and shirts with no pockets. Sly noticed Sidney's agitation.

'Smoker are you, Mr Lambert?'

'Yes, you got one?'

'No, Mr Lambert, I am a member of ASH.'

Sly was very pleased. 'Shouldn't take long to break him down,' he thought. 'Couple of hours of nicotine withdrawal should do it.'

143

41 Coventry Says Goodbye

The taxi had circumnavigated the airport three times. 'Round again, please,' shouted Coventry.

'Bleedin' hell, I'm goin' dizzy!' moaned the driver.

'Oh, stop whining and drive. You're getting paid for it, aren't you?'

She slammed the sliding window shut. The children were astonished at the authority in their mother's voice. Where had it come from? A week ago she would have apologized to the driver for causing his vertiginous bout. Now, here she was involved in a clandestine meeting arranged by a mysterious, posh woman dressed entirely in black.

Coventry sat between the children, with an arm gripped tight round each of their shoulders. In ten minutes she had to return to the airport. She explained her dilemma to the children.

'I promised Dodo I'd go back. I *think* she's planning our escape route, to Wales.'

'How long would you get in the nick – if you gave yourself up?' asked Mary.

John answered, 'I asked Dad. He reckons 'bout four years; with time off for good behaviour.'

'Mum *would* behave, wouldn't you, Mum?'

Coventry kissed her daughter's neck, but said, 'I'd *die* in prison, Mary.'

'You could carry on going to art classes in prison though, couldn't you?' blurted John.

'You read my diary! Oh John, you didn't, you didn't read my diary?'

'Sorry, Mum, but I didn't want the law to find it.'

'No, you're right. You must think I'm mad.'

'No I don't,' insisted John.

'What diary?' asked Mary.

'Bradford Keynes thinks you're a magic painter.'

'Does he?'

'Who's Bradford Keynes?' asked Mary.

'He was a friend of mine,' said Coventry, who had stopped being

144

infatuated with Bradford on her second visit to the art classes at the Workers' Educational Institute.

Mary was crying. 'Mum, can we come with you to Wales or wherever you're going?'

Coventry said, 'You can't miss school. *You've* got to get your exams; and Dad needs you!'

John said, 'What will we do without you?'

Coventry said, 'You'll grow up and then we'll be together again somewhere.'

It was a dreadful moment for them all when the cab arrived back at the rank. After Coventry had paid the driver they clung together in a tight-knit family group, each one reluctant to let go of the other two.

Detective Sergeant Horsefield watched them with great sadness. He had been watching them since he'd heard the announcement calling for John Dakin. His own cab driver had been thrilled to be told to 'follow that cab'. It was a cliché he had waited seventeen years to hear.

Horsefield should have approached Coventry immediately, arrested her and then sat back and waited for the congratulations, the admiring publicity and the inevitable promotion; but the longer he watched the little group, the more reluctant he became to break it up. He prayed to God for guidance and strength.

God advised him to leave the police force and apply to join the priesthood. So Horsefield turned his back on his career and went back to the Arrivals lounge, where he found Ruth Lambert sitting on a bench surrounded by luggage and broken Portuguese folk art plates. She looked exactly like the photograph he carried in his pocket. Small, anorexic build and snaggled teeth.

'She must have *something*,' thought Horsefield charitably, for he also had a photograph of Sidney's dazzling features secreted about his person.

'Mrs Ruth Lambert?'

'Yes.'

'I'm a policeman [though not for long, not for bloody long!]. Your niece and nephew have come to meet you; they're outside, near the cab rank. I'll watch your luggage for you.'

42 Practicalities

Podger's official car, containing Podger, Nicholas Cutbush and a Secret Service officer called Natasha Krantz, drove into a VIP entrance at the back of the airport and parked.

Podger was still distraught. Before the car arrived he had told his wife everything; about Jaffa, about his mistress, and about other marital and financial infidelities. Once he'd started he couldn't stop. To his surprise his patrician wife had gone berserk and attacked him in his own bathtub. She had screamed and had hysterics and turned the shower attachment on and directed scalding water onto his unprotected genitals. With vicious malignity she had shouted, 'Don't expect *me* to stand by you and play the brave little woman and be photographed hand in hand with you walking on the lawn. There's no *way* we're going to pose for the press patting the sodding Labrador, you bastard! If this scandal breaks I shall sue for divorce. I'm not cut out for martyrdom! I will not do a Mary Archer!'

Podger had smeared Vaseline onto his sore pink genitals under his wife's Medusa-like gaze. He wouldn't have minded being turned to stone then and there. Anything was better than getting through the days that lay ahead. He had an appointment with the PM in the morning. They were to discuss law and order. His penis shrivelled at the thought.

With his companions Podger got out of the car and shuffled painfully along corridors, and then into a VIP ante-room where Dodo was waiting, as had previously been arranged.

'What's wrong, Podgie?' said Dodo. 'You look as though you've pooed your pants.'

Podger lowered his haunches into a chair with great circumspection. He wished that he had taken his genitalia to a doctor, but there had been no time and anyway wouldn't the mutual embarrassment be even more painful than the scalds? The celebrity of his face seemed to make the ordinariness of his sexual organs harder to bear. Nicholas ordered the Security officer to check the room for listening devices and hidden cameras. Natasha Krantz appeared to do a thorough job, even to the extent of fetching step-ladders and unscrewing the recessed lighting in the ceiling. Nobody spoke until she said, ''Sclean, sir.'

'Now check my sister.'

Natasha set her face and frisked Dodo.

'Clean, sir.'

'Where's your murdering friend?' said Nicholas.

'She'll be here soon,' replied Dodo. Then, 'Have you brought everything I asked for, Nick?'

Natasha Krantz opened her brief-case and took out bundles of money and various documents. Dodo opened her black bag and gave Ms Krantz the passport photographs and Ms Krantz began to change the official identities of Coventry and Dodo. Their new names were suited to their class and accents. Dodo became Miss Angela Stafford-Clark, birthplace: Leamington Spa; and Coventry was about to mutate into Ms Suzanne Lowe, birthplace: Nottingham.

43 Parting

It was Natasha Krantz who parted me from my children.

'You must come now! Now! Say goodbye and come!'

She peeled their hands away from my waist and neck and, very sternly, said: 'You did not see your mother tonight, did you?'

They shook their lovely blond heads.

'And you did not see me?'

Again they shook their heads.

'Now say goodbye to your mother; she must go.'

Splinters in the brain.

44 The Sun Rises in the East

'Please don't cry, Jaffa darling. I can't bear it. Nicholas, give her your handkerchief.'

'It's *silk*, it's not meant to be used.'

Podger proffered his and I took it and covered my face in white linen. I could look nobody in the eye. I had turned my back on nature. I was an outcast, a pariah. Murder was a mere triviality compared to my most recent outrageous act. That of leaving my children.

Dodo forced something between my fingers, thin, hard, rectangular. I removed the handkerchief and saw a navy book. I opened it and read my new name: Ms Suzanne Lowe, birthplace: Nottingham. The pages of Suzanne's passport were stamped with visas to America and Australia and India.

'Did you do the impossible, Podger?' said Dodo. Podger indicated that Natasha Krantz would speak for him.

'Yes, it was done.' She handed Dodo some sheets of paper. Dodo looked at them and sighed.

'Wonderful, thank you. When does it leave?'

Natasha said, 'They owe us a favour, they have diverted a plane from Paris. You will be most unpopular with the other passengers. Now, where is the photo?'

Dodo gave Podger the polaroid photograph that had caused so much trouble. He tried to tear it in half, gave up and sat with it on his painful lap.

'You have copies, of course,' said Podger.

'Of course,' replied Dodo. 'They're in the post.'

'You fucking little cow, you've ruined my marriage and probably my career.' Podger's eyes sparkled with angry tears. He put the photograph into an ashtray and set fire to it. We all watched as the image twisted and melted and eventually turned in on itself.

Dodo said: 'Cheer up, Podger old love; you've still got the mistress and the bank balance, not to mention the English Establishment behind you. Things could be worse.'

'We should have had them killed,' burst out Nick. 'None of us will sleep easy in our beds ever again.'

I know that I got on a bus and then a plane; and that I felt the plane accelerate, then rise, bank and turn towards the East. I remember looking out of the little window and seeing the airport lights in the far distance. Somewhere, down there, were my children, preparing to go home. And down there with them, now left behind, were Miss Coventry Lambert, my parents' daughter; Mrs Derek Dakin, my husband's wife; Margaret Dakin, my son's invention; Lauren McSkye, Bradford Keynes's student; and Jaffa, Dodo's friend.

'Where are we going?' asked Suzanne Lowe.

'To Moscow,' was the unexpected reply.

45 Edna Dakin Takes to the Road

Coventry's mother-in-law, Edna Dakin, was only half listening to her son Derek. The other half of her attention was focused on the street outside where, as usual, nothing was happening. She saw another woman of her own age group looking forlornly out of her window. Edna thought, 'It's these awful buildings; they've put a spell on us, a dreary grey spell. Why haven't we got colours and patterns and plants that grow up walls like they have abroad? No wonder we don't want to walk about in the ugly plain streets they've built for us.

'And that new community centre!' Edna scoffed. 'Nasty low echoing concrete thing *that* is. I used to work in a laundry which was more comfortable and pretty than that.' Edna felt a huge rage swell inside her chest as she looked out upon the rows of identical concrete houses stretching down the hill. 'No wonder the kids broke the young trees,' she thought. 'It's because they can't wait for them to grow.

'And those terrible shops! Which they call a *Parade*, a parade of shops. Ha! But a parade is a nice thing, a celebration. You wave a flag at a parade. You don't buy your groceries at one. And why is there nowhere for children to play?' asked Edna in her mind. 'They ought at least to learn how to play before they go on the dole.'

'Mum, are you listening?'

She turned her slummocky body round to face her son. What a little runt he was! How did he end up with Coventry, so beautiful that she turned heads where'er she walked? Like the song.

'Mum, you're making a noise.'

'I'm humming an old song: "Where'er she walks, cool vales . . ." '

'But we're having a conversation . . .'

'No, we're not, Derek. It takes two to have a conversation and, as usual, you're talking and I'm forced to listen.'

'Mum! Aren't you well?'

'I'm as well as somebody can be who's bored out of her bleedin' brains.'

'Mum! I've never heard you use bad language before.'

'Oh, I use it quite a bit when I'm on my own indoors. I 'eff and blind like mad. I enjoy swearing.'

'You're not well, are you? It's all this worry about Coventry, isn't it?'

'Funny Derek, but I'm not worried about her at all. I'm sort of pleased for her. I wish I'd done the same.'

'What! Murdered someone?'

'No. The running away bit. I mean, *it's exciting*, isn't it? She could be anywhere: Timbuctoo, Constantinople, Land's End, anywhere. Better than living round here and going to the shops once a day. I've decided I hate my life, Derek. I'm having a go at changing it.'

'How?'

'Well, for a start, I'm having driving lessons.'

'Driving lessons? You'll kill yourself!'

'No I won't. I'm quite a sensible woman, and there *is* such a thing as dual controls, you know.'

'It's ridiculous. How can you afford a car? You're a pensioner.'

'When I pass my test, I'll cash in my funeral insurance.'

'You can't do that, what about the coffin you wanted – and the mourners' cars? And the sit-down funeral tea?'

Mrs Dakin laughed at the panic-stricken expression on her son's face. 'Let the council burn me up. I've paid 'em enough rates over the years.'

A car hooter sounded outside. Derek got up and went to the window. A driving school car was parked at the kerb. A young man was settling himself into the passenger seat.

'That'll be him,' said Mrs Dakin. She turned the gas fire off, picked up her handbag and went into the hall.

''Bye Derek,' she said, pointedly.

They left the house together. Derek walked away without looking back.

He heard an engine revving fiercely, then the driving school car accelerated past him with his old mother at the wheel. She papped the hooter and waved. Derek watched as the car vanished over the brow of the hill. In his opinion the car was exceeding the speed limit by at least fifteen miles an hour. He made a note of the name of the driving school: Surepass. He would telephone them when he got home and report the instructor who was supposed to be teaching his mother to obey the laws of the road.

Derek wondered why all the women he knew appeared to be going mad. It wasn't just members of his own family. The girls at work were getting stroppy: demanding things, more money, improved conditions, flexi-hours. And hadn't women's voices got louder? Weren't their clothes gaudier and their bodies taller and more imposing? Derek lumbered home, like a dinosaur unhappily parted from its swamp, uneasily sensing that the climate was changing.

Epilogue

Six months to the day have passed since Coventry ran away from her home and family. Since then a Russian Christmas card has arrived at Badger's Copse Close addressed to 'the children'. There was no message. The inside of the card was completely blank, but the children knew who it was from.

RUTH   Has stopped taking her contraceptive pills. Sidney doesn't know. Ruth will not inform him until she is twenty-nine weeks' pregnant.

SIDNEY   Has been promoted: he is now Area Manager for the East Midlands, a total of thirty-seven stores. Since his promotion sales figures have increased dramatically. One of Sidney's first recommendations to head office was that all references to 'Shops' should be changed to 'Centres'.

HORSEFIELD   Is living in a caravan with Barbara and Matthew just outside Cambridge. He attends a theological college. He is very happy, he doesn't know that Barbara isn't.

PODGER   Thinks about Coventry as soon as he opens his eyes in the morning. He is alone in the double bed. His wife has left him and is living with a Labour candidate. One of Podger's arteries is furring up. He doesn't know this, and won't until the blood fails to get through to his heart on 2 August 1992.

DEREK   Has had a triumph. Naomi won him Best of Show at a United Kingdom tortoise convention. Derek's and Naomi's pictures appeared in the local paper, under the unfortunate headline, 'Fugitive's husband comes out of his shell'. There is a woman, a certain Mrs Daphne Pye, who is very interested in Derek. She thinks he is a marvellous conversationalist. Daphne is a tortoise fancier, she can do the foxtrot and she is a non-smoker.

MARY   Has turned into a beauty, she works hard at school, she thinks about her mother constantly.

JOHN   Is retaking his A levels. He has also turned into a beauty.

EDNA DAKIN   Passed her driving test at her first attempt. She bought a left-hand drive Vauxhall Chevette in metallic blue. It cost her two hundred and fifty pounds. She is hardly ever to be found at home.

SLY   Is dead. He burnt to death on the M1 motorway on his way back from Gatwick. It is believed he fell asleep at the wheel. All documents pertaining to Coventry Dakin were destroyed in the fire.